At first Albion thought it was a bundle of rags. But then the bundle of rags rolled over and cried out. Albion threw up and Nelson's hands shook so badly he almost fired a burst from his weapon.

"Good Jesus Christ, it's a man," Nelson said.

Albion's stomach was churning, but he could not take his eyes off the hideous sight on the road. It was a man, or what was left of one. His hair was gone, his eyes bulged nearly out of their sockets, and his swollen tongue protruded from his mouth. The worst part were the sores which made his face, neck and hands look like hamburger.

"Beta canister . . . they made me do it. . ." the man said, his voice barely a whisper.

"What's he—" Albion started to say, when the man on the driveway suddenly arched his back, let out a scream and then slumped back dead, blood oozing from his mouth where he had bitten through his tongue.

NICK CARTER IS IT!

"Nick Carter out-Bonds James Bond."
                    —*Buffalo Evening News*

"Nick Carter is America's #1 espionage agent."
                    —*Variety*

"Nick Carter is razor-sharp suspense."
                    —*King Features*

"Nick Carter is extraordinarily big."
                    —*Bestsellers*

"Nick Carter has attracted an army of addicted readers . . . the books are fast, have plenty of action and just the right degree of sex . . . Nick Carter is the American James Bond, suave, sophisticated, a killer with both the ladies and the enemy."
                    —*The New York Times*

NICK CARTER

THE STRONTIUM CODE

CHARTER
NEW YORK

A Division of Charter Communications Inc.
A GROSSET & DUNLAP COMPANY
51 Madison Avenue
New York, New York 10010

First Ace Charter Printing September 1981
Published simultaneously in Canada
Manufactured in the United States of America
    2 4 6 8 0 9 7 5 3 1

THE STRONTIUM CODE

Dedicated to the men of the
Secret Services of the
United States of America

PROLOGUE

The noonday sun beat unmercifully on the piles of modernistic glass and concrete that was Al Kuwait—Kuwait City—the capital of the oil rich sheikdom of Kuwait.

Pfc Lawrence Albion snuck a look out the doorway of the guard hut, across the compound toward the front entrance of the U.S. Embassy. The parking lot was nearly deserted at this time of the day, and Albion knew that most of the staff would not be back until well after three in the afternoon.

Until then there'd be no chickenshit, no one to look over their shoulders and no one to mind if a man had a quick smoke.

He ducked back inside the guard shack and nodded at his friend Jigs, the other Marine guard. "All clear," he said.

Jigs—Corporal Donald Nelson—grinned broadly as he put his foot up on the chair, pulled a crumpled pack of Camels from the elastic in his sock and shook one out, offering it to Albion.

When both men had lit up, Albion checked outside again; the parking lot was still clear and the Beneid al-Gar was nearly free of traffic. Almost

1

everything outside came to a grinding halt during the midday in high summer.

Inside the hut it was one hundred degrees, but outside in the direct glare of the sun it was easily twenty degrees warmer.

"Twenty-nine days," Albion said smugly.

Jigs nodded. "Short timer, that's what you are." He made the comment solemnly, as if it was the most important thing he had ever said. Neither man was over twenty-two. "What's the first thing you're going to do when you get home, Larry?"

Albion had thought about this almost from the first week he had been assigned embassy duty in Kuwait nearly three years ago. "I'm going down to Colorado, to Estes Park. It'll be the middle of August, but that's all right, 'cause at ten thousand feet there'll still be snow. I'm goin' to have my girl with me, and the both of us are going to take off all our clothes and jump into the biggest goddamned pile of snow we can—"

An unearthly, animalistic scream stopped Albion in mid-sentence, and for a moment he looked from Jigs to the door and back to Jigs.

"What in the hell . . ." he started, but Nelson had thrown down his cigarette, had grabbed his carbine from where it was leaning against the desk and was out the door, levering a round into the chamber.

A moment later Albion had crushed his cigarette out in an ashtray, had withdrawn his .45 automatic and had snapped the ejector slide back as he burst out the door.

The bright sun and intense heat hit him like a blast furnace, causing him to reel back for a moment and squint his eyes. Then he saw the thing laying in the driveway a couple of yards beyond Jigs.

At first Albion thought it was a bundle of rags. When he noticed blood and what appeared to be raw meat, the bile rose up in his stomach. Someone had evidently killed an animal, wrapped the carcass in filthy rags and dumped it here.

But then the bundle of rags rolled over and cried out. Albion threw up and Nelson's hands shook so badly he almost fired a burst from his weapon.

"Good Jesus Christ, it's a man," Nelson said.

Albion's stomach was churning, but he could not take his eyes off the hideous sight on the road. It was a man, or what was left of one. His hair was gone, his eyes bulged nearly out of their sockets, and his swollen tongue protruded from his mouth. The worst part were the sores which made his face, neck and hands look like hamburger.

Nelson was in a half crouch, his left foot slightly forward, his carbine out in the defensive posture as he scanned the street and the buildings on the other side.

"Get the medics out here on the double," he shouted without bothering to look around.

The man on the driveway screamed again, the sound high pitched and keening, cutting into Albion's abject terror.

"Sonofabitching Arabs," he said half under his breath. He was frightened for his own life. "Sonofabitching . . . ."

"Larry, for Christ's sake," Nelson shouted. "Get the medics! Move it, man!"

Albion turned and, half stumbling over his own feet, raced into the guard shack, grabbing the telephone with trembling hands.

"U.S. Embassy," the operator said pleasantly.

"Front gate alert," Albion shouted into the phone. "We need a medic and guards. *On the double!*"

He slammed the phone back on its cradle and went outside, just as Nelson was getting down on one knee next to the creature on the driveway.

"Jigs?" he said starting forward. Albion did not want to get very close to the thing on the road. Even at this distance he could smell the sweet, cloying odor of rotted flesh.

"Beta canister," the man on the driveway cried clearly. He reached out his right hand and grabbed Nelson by the sleeve of his clean khaki uniform. Nelson jerked back involuntarily, leaving a wide red streak down his sleeve from the man's blood.

"Jesus," Nelson said, stumbling back in disgust.

"Beta canister," the dying man whispered loudly. "*Akai Maru*. Beta canister . . . they made me do it."

"What'd he say?" Albion asked.

Nelson glanced back at his friend, and shook his head. "I don't know," he mumbled. He looked beyond Albion. "Where the hell are those medics?"

"Beta canister . . . they made me do it . . ." the man said, his voice barely a whisper now. Yet Albion who stood a half a dozen yards away could hear him clearly. "Beta canister . . . *Akai Maru* . . ."

"What's he—" Albion started to say, when the man on the driveway suddenly arched his back, let out a scream and then slumped back dead, blood oozing from his mouth where he had bitten through his tongue.

ONE

It was snowing lightly and a cold wind blew directly down the dirty alley, the harsh overhead light atop the building at the corner shining directly in my eyes as I watched the back entrance. In the distance somewhere I could hear the sounds of traffic and what sounded like the clanging of bells.

Christmas? I asked myself, concentrating a moment on the melancholy sounds.

The door burst open, and in one swift motion I stepped away from the wooden crate I had been hiding behind, dropped to one knee and brought my Luger up, snapping the safety catch off.

Too late I saw the motion atop the building out of the corner of my eye, suddenly something very hard slammed into my shoulder and I was thrown backward, my gun going off harmlessly overhead.

"End exercise," a loudspeaker blared. The snow stopped, the wind died to nothing and the overhead lights came up as Stan Philips the training officer limped around the corner on his artificial legs, a huge grin on his face.

I picked myself up off the floor, dusted myself off and holstered my training weapon that fired relatively harmless soft rubber bullets. There would be a couple of bruises on my body where I had taken the two hits, but what hurt even more was my failure.

One of Philips's training technicians was standing atop the building by the corner now, and he waved as he holstered his weapon. The man was dressed all in black and with the strong light he had hidden behind he had been totally invisible.

Still, I told myself, I should have known. If this had been for real I'd be dead now, not standing here waiting for Philips who'd chuckle about this for the next day or so.

"The Christmas bells were a nice touch," I said beating the man to the punch. He always had something smart to say.

I had a great respect for Philips who had been Killmaster training officer for as long as I had had the designation N/3. Agency scuttlebutt had it that he had been one of the original licensed-to-kill agents with the OSS, had later been swallowed up in the CIA's Clandestine Operations section and finally had been recruited to AXE when it was formed.

He had been tumbled in Czechoslovakia in the early sixties, had been captured, tortured and nearly killed, yet somehow he had managed to escape with most of his body and all of his mind intact.

The man deserved and got much respect from all of us. But he did have a perverse sense of humor.

He stuck out his leather-clad metal hand and I shook it, waiting for the squeeze, but it never came. "You should have expected the man on the roofline. The light was a perfect Class I."

I shrugged. "We learn from our mistakes?"

"Bullshit," Philips said genially. He took my

arm and led me down the alley, around the corner to the wide metal door which he banged open and we were outside, the hot Arizona sun beating down on us.

I had been here at AXE's rest, recuperation and training ranch outside Phoenix, Arizona for three weeks and felt as fit as I had ever felt.

"David called about ten minutes ago," Philips said as we headed across the compound toward billeting and transportation. "He wants you in D.C. *post haste.*"

"An assignment?" I asked. David Hawk is the iron-willed chief of AXE, the super-secret agency formed shortly after the McCarthy witch hunts which had sounded the death knell for effective clandestine operations by the Central Intelligence Agency. Although McCarthy believed there was a Communist under every bedspring, he also believed that every government agency, even the CIA was riddled with Reds, and therefore had to be watched closely.

The CIA did its thing   seek out, gather, collate and analyze data, while we were commissioned to do our thing—covert action.

"I don't know," Philips said. "He didn't take me into his confidence, although he did ask how you were doing."

"What'd you tell him?" I asked.

Philips grinned again. "I told him you were as fit as you'd ever be. But that was before this last exercise." He laughed out loud this time.

I couldn't think of a thing to say and we went the rest of the way across the compound in silence. When we reached the long, low modern building that contained transient officers' quarters, Philips stopped at the entrance.

"Your things have been packed for you and a driver will be around in a couple of minutes to get you out to the airport."

"Did he give you any hints?" I asked.

Philips looked at me, a serious expression on his face. "Only one," he said. "And it better not get back to him."

I waited.

"You'll be back here within twenty-four hours. Possibly sooner."

"Back here?"

Philips nodded. "We've got a couple of things to teach you."

"Then you do know what my assignment is," I said.

"No, I don't, Nick, and that's the truth. All David told me was that he needed you in D.C. immediately, but that he'd be sending you back here for a special equipment briefing."

"What kind of equipment?" I asked, but Philips shook his head.

"That's as far as I'm going. You'll find out when you get back," he said.

"Thanks," I replied dryly.

"Have a good trip."

We shook hands and I went inside where the orderly handed me my suitcase, my travel voucher and plane tickets; a few minutes later my transportation arrived.

It was five o'clock in the evening by the time my plane touched down at Washington's National Airport and 6:30 P.M. by the time I had retrieved my suitcase, hailed a cab and made it to Dupont Circle at the junction of Massachusetts, New Hampshire and Connecticut Avenues.

The front for AXE's worldwide operations is the Amalgamated Press and Wire Services, and as an actual news service our organization ranks only slightly behind the Associated Press, United Press International and Reuters. But the press service has always been nothing more than a cover for our actual operations.

I checked my suitcase with the security guard on the first floor and took the elevator up to the fourth, where Hawk has his offices, and was shown immediately inside.

David Hawk had his feet propped up on the windowsill, his coat off, his tie loose and his sleeves rolled up as he stared at the Dupont Plaza Hotel across the street and beyond it to the north, the Argentine Embassy. A halo of cigar smoke wreathed his head, and when he turned around I was shocked at the harried expression in his normally placid eyes.

I had been in this cluttered office more times than I care to count. I had faced this man for assignments in crises that threatened the safety of the world. But never had I seen him so apparently distracted, so agitated. It was disquieting.

"I'm glad you could make it so quickly, Nick," he said, his voice soft. "Have a seat."

As I came across the room and sat down in a chair opposite his littered desk, he reached forward and buzzed his secretary.

"I want this floor red-lighted for the next hour," he told her.

"Yes, sir," his secretary's voice came over the intercom.

"Put the blind on the phone lines, bring the scanners up and hold the elevator as well," he added.

"Yes, sir," the secretary replied, surprise evident in her voice.

Hawk then sat back and stared at me for several long seconds, although I doubt that he was actually seeing me. After a while he blinked, took the cigar from his mouth and laid it in an overflowing ashtray.

"Before I start, I'm going to tell you two things and then give you the option to accept or decline."

I held my silence, but my heart was accelerating. What he was saying to me was extraordinary, but I had a feeling what he was going to tell me was going to be even more unusual. Killmasters were not usually given a choice in their assignments.

"First of all, this job is as important as it is delicate; second, it's exceedingly dangerous. Probably more dangerous than anything we've ever done. Your option is to take it or leave it."

"I'll take it, whatever it—" I started to say, but he had anticipated my reaction and held me off.

"You'd better wait until I finish briefing you before you make that choice," he said. He flipped open a file folder in front of him on the desk, extracted a couple of Wirephoto pictures, then handed them to me.

My stomach turned over. Both photographs showed the barely recognizable remains of a human being. A man, I presumed, although it was hard to tell. His head was hairless, his eyes bulged nearly out of their sockets, his tongue protruded from his mouth, and his entire body was covered with open sores.

"Was he burned?" I asked.

"Radioactive poisoning," Hawk said. I handed

the photos back and he slid them into the file folder without looking at them. "Whoever takes this assignment could easily end up the same way."

I shuddered involuntarily. "What are our options?"

"We don't have any."

"Then you'd better tell me everything, sir," I said.

Hawk stared at me a little while longer, then sighed deeply and sat back in his chair. "Eight o'clock our time last night the poor devil in those photographs collapsed at the front gate of our embassy in Kuwait City. Before he died the Marine guards at the gate said the man spoke several words." He sat forward again, opened the file folder and withdrew a sheet of paper, then read from it.

"Beta canister . . . beta canister . . . *Akai Maru* . . . beta canister . . . they made me do it . . . beta canister . . . they made me do it . . . beta canister . . . *Akai Maru.*" He put the paper back in the file. "Those were the man's exact words. Moments later he died."

"The *Akai Maru* is a ship or a person?"

"A ship," Hawk said. "She's an oil tanker. A super tanker. Libyan registry, belonging to a Japanese consortium out of Yokohama. She left Kuwait City two days ago with five million gallons of crude oil bound for Bakersfield, California."

"And a beta canister?" I asked.

Hawk licked his lips, something I had never seen him do before, and then he picked up his cigar and re-lit it.

"A beta canister is a standard packaging unit for strontium 90," he said, his voice barely audible. "It weighs a hundred pounds, nearly all of which is lead shielding."

"Strontium 90," I repeated, thinking of the photographs of the badly burned man.

"Highly radioactive," Hawk continued. "Half life of twenty-eight years, which means it'll stay dangerous for at least a hundred years. It's used in some nuclear reactors and it's the by-product of a nuclear explosion."

"The man in the photographs? He handled the stuff?" I asked.

"Presumably," Hawk said.

"Who was he?"

"We don't know yet. They're still trying to identify him out there. He was an Arab though."

"Where'd he get the material?"

"We don't know that either. There shouldn't be anything like that anywhere in the Mideast."

Suddenly what Hawk was telling me struck hard. "The *Akai Maru*. The strontium 90 is aboard the tanker? And she's bounded for California?"

"We don't know. But it's a fair assumption."

"Why don't we just stop the ship in international waters, board her and take the canister?" I asked.

"The President vetoed that idea for a number of reasons. First of all the ship is Japanese, and if our Navy did such a thing it would be piracy and possibly be construed as an act of war. Secondly, if the crew, or part of the crew, is in on this, they could just dump the canister overboard before we got to it. Then there would be serious trouble. One canister of strontium 90 would, I'm told, be enough to pollute the entire Indian Ocean."

I had a feeling I knew what was coming and I didn't like it very much.

"And finally," Hawk was saying, "even if the Navy was successful, we would never find out where it came from or where it was going."

"Mind if I smoke, sir?" I asked.

"Go ahead," Hawk nodded, and as I was lighting myself a cigarette, he took out a bottle of brandy and two glasses from a desk drawer and poured two healthy shots, offering me one. I had never seen Hawk drink in his office before. But I wasn't about to argue with him.

I took mine and drank it. He poured me another. He didn't put the bottle away. Instead he picked up his glass, drained it and poured himself a second.

"You understand what you'd be up against?" he said softly.

I nodded, sipping at my second drink. The liquor did nothing to ease the knot that had formed in my stomach.

"You want to accept the assignment?"

Again I nodded.

"We have to accomplish four things. First: Find out where the strontium 90 came from; no one in the Mideast should have access to anything like it. Second: Find out who placed it aboard the *Akai Maru*, if it's there; we're sure the man who stumbled into our embassy was not alone in this. Third: Find out what its ultimate destination and purpose are. And finally: Steal it."

"All that without upsetting the Japanese," I added.

Hawk nodded. "Or upsetting the delicate balance among OPEC."

"How about time?" I asked. "The ship has already been at sea for forty-eight hours."

A dark expression crossed Hawk's features. "I

just don't know, Nick. There are too many factors to consider. If it was just a matter of intercepting the ship and taking the canister off before it reached California, we'd have plenty of time. She's got another eighteen days before she's due to dock."

"What's her route?" I asked.

"Gulf of Aden, Red Sea, through the Suez into the Med, and from there across the Atlantic and through the Panama Canal to California. But that's not the problem."

I waited for him to continue.

"We're keeping pretty close tabs on the ship—from a distance—to make sure no other vessel approaches her. But if whoever placed the canister aboard the ship finds out one of their people told our embassy about it, there could be immediate trouble."

There was something else though. I could see it in his eyes. Something even more important. "And?" I asked softly.

He looked at me for a long moment. "Beta canisters, under normal handling procedures, *do not leak.*"

I shrugged. "So what . . ." I started to say, but then a cold chill went right through me. "Jesus," I said.

Hawk nodded. "The man is dead. Radioactive poisoning. Either the canister leaked or they opened it for some reason."

And that was the real problem I would be facing, I thought grimly. Even if I carried a sensitive Geiger counter, I could stumble across the canister. And then it would be too late for me. I'd end up just like the poor devil in the photographs.

"The Navy will be standing by out there to help you," Hawk was saying, and I looked up out of my thoughts at him. "They'll give you anything you need, anywhere you want it, at any time."

"I'll be boarding the tanker?"

"That's up to you, Nick," Hawk said. "It depends upon what you're able to come up with in Kuwait."

"I don't suppose there'd be a cover for me. Some way for me to legitimately board her?"

Hawk shook his head. "We can't do anything to create even the slightest suspicion that we're on to the fact the beta canister is aboard."

"We don't know that it is aboard."

"No," Hawk admitted. "But we're assuming it is. It's up to you to make sure."

I stood up. "Philips said I was supposed to return for special equipment training."

Hawk looked up and then handed the file to me. "Take this along with you. Political affairs had added some material on the Mideast situation, including some stuff on local terrorist groups."

I took the file.

"Read it when you get the chance. Philips has some radiation detection equipment for you, and I want you to spend some time on boarding procedures. It won't be easy."

"No," I said. "I'll take the morning flight down."

"Go on out to Andrews immediately. They've got transportation for you," Hawk said. "And turn your weapons over to the armorer downstairs, he'll see that they get in the diplomatic bag for Kuwait this evening. They'll be waiting for you at the embassy."

At the door I stopped and turned back. "Do you suppose they want to build a bomb?"

"I don't know, Nick. But so far there has never been a real act of international terrorism in the continental United States. We all want to keep it that way."

"As soon as I start snooping around it could tip them off."

Hawk nodded. "Be careful, Nick. Come back."

Philips was waiting for me when I got back to the R and R facility and he didn't give me a chance to unpack or even to rest. I was given a set of dark coveralls, thin leather gloves and soft rubber-soled shoes; then I was immediately driven by jeep out into the desert at least five miles from the main compound.

It was after two o'clock in the morning and the sky was moonless and nearly pitch black when we finally pulled up and parked a hundred yards from the strangest conglomeration of scaffolding, telephone poles and what appeared to be gigantic propellers that I had ever seen.

"What the hell is it?" I asked, peering across the desert at what looked like a metal billboard that rose sixty or seventy feet above the ground.

"An oil tanker in a relatively calm sea making twenty-four knots into a headwind of sixteen knots," Philips said. "It was the best we could do in such short notice."

A dozen technicians were standing by as we got out of the jeep and went the rest of the way on foot to the base of the mammoth structure. On either side of the metal wall, were tall, well-guyed telephone poles on which were attached electric motors driving huge fan blades.

Directly in front of the structure was a narrow platform—about ten feet above the ground and nearly twenty yards away from the wall—that curved in from the base to a point two thirds of the way up and then curved sharply outward.

At the top right corner of the monstrous wall, was a large white light that shone only to the right, offering no illumination whatsoever behind it.

A thick rope snaked down from the top of the wall to the low platform which we had approached.

Philips looked up at the formidable wall, then down at the platform, and finally shook his head.

"The problem presented to me was to get you aboard a supertanker at sea without detection," he said. "We couldn't bring you in by air, nor could we give you one of NASA's rocket belts. In either you'd be picked up on radar, if not visually."

One of his technicians was coming from the back of a canvas-covered truck, lugging what looked like some kind of a safety harness, as well as a large backpack.

"The only way is over the top," I said.

"That's right," Philips agreed. "From the conning tower hatch of a partially submerged submarine." He slapped a leather-clad metal hand against the platform supports. "Twenty yards is as close as the sub can get to the ship because of the tanker's bulbous underwater bow. And even at that distance it'll be cutting it close. If the seas are rough, they might have to stand off as far as fifty or sixty yards, in which case your fifty-fifty chance of survival would drop to something like eighty-twenty or maybe even ninety-ten."

"Great," I said softly.

Philips smiled wryly. "We've all been through that sort of thing before," he said.

His technician came up and Philips introduced us. "Nick Carter, Stan Fenster. He'll be running your briefing and coordinating the simulation team."

We shook hands after the man dumped the pack on the ground. "We're going to hook you up to a safety line this morning," he said briskly. "Although for the real McCoy you won't have that luxury, of course. Turn around."

"Of course," I said, and I did as I was told. Fenster strapped the safety harness over my shoulders, around my waist and then between my legs. All the snaps ended at a large mountain climber's swivel snap at my chest.

"The pack weighs forty-seven pounds," Fenster was saying as he picked it up. "This morning it's filled with rocks, but your mission equipment will include a powerful radiation detector, a radiation-safe suit, bulky but light, a shortwave transceiver, an Uzo lightweight machine gun with seven spare clips of forty-five rounds each, and of course rations."

He helped me strap the pack on, and as I adjusted to the feel of it, I looked up again at the wall and tried to imagine climbing it, not here on the desert, but out at sea; perhaps with a swell running, wet, cold, and moving through the water at more than twenty knots.

"What do you think?" Philips asked.

"Doesn't matter," I said glancing at him. "Let's get on with it."

"Very good," Fenster said, and I was sure I detected a note of pleasure in his voice.

He climbed up onto the ten-foot platform, which represented the height out of the water that the sub's conning tower would be, and I followed him.

When I reached the top he was loading a squat, very deadly looking shotgun with a large shell. Sticking out of the barrel was the end of a padded grappling hook, connected to a coil of thin wire.

"This is the grappling hook launcher, fires a two-gauge shotgun shell," Fenster was saying. "It won't, however, be your responsibility. The Navy will do it for you."

Fenster turned, braced the shotgun firmly against his shoulder and, aiming up toward the top of the wall sixty feet above us, pulled the trigger. The roar was deafening and the recoil almost knocked him flat on his back. I smiled.

The grappling hook shot up and over the top of the wall, the thin wire whining off the spool. A second later Fenster had recovered his balance and had reeled up the slack, snapping two sets of foot-and-hand grips to the wire.

"Release the trigger on either grip and the jaws will loosen from the wire and you can slide it upward, setting it in place. Transfer your body weight to the upper grips, release the lower set and slide it up. And so forth. It's just like climbing a ladder."

"Almost," I said, and he glanced sharply at me.

"Any questions?" he asked.

I shook my head.

He handed me the grips and I tugged against the line. It seemed firm.

"This morning you'll be hooked up to a safety line—" Fenster started to say, but I shook my head and he stopped in mid-sentence.

"I don't want to depend upon something I won't have during the real thing," I said. My mouth was dry and the pack at my back seemed to have doubled in weight over the last few seconds.

Fenster smiled. "Very well," he said. "The fan blades will produce an unsteady wind of twenty-five knots, gusting at times to forty knots. It'll help simulate the real thing."

I nodded.

"Good luck then," he said. He had a walkie-talkie strapped to his belt and he reached down and hit the transmit button twice. A moment later the huge fan blades on the telephone poles started up with a clatter. Within a few seconds we were engulfed in a windstorm that at times threatened to sweep us both off the platform and made talking totally impossible.

I glanced at Fenster who was grinning. He gave me the thumbs up sign, clapped me on the back and then stood aside.

For a long moment I remained where I was, gauging the strength of the wind, the weight of my backpack and my hold on the wire grips; but then I slid the mechanisms up as high on the wire as I could reach, got up on the rail and jumped off.

The wind gusted at that moment, blowing me far to the left. I just managed to swivel my body around again and get my feet out and set, when I slammed into the side of the metal-clad wall.

And then I was climbing for my life, fighting the grips every foot of the way, the backpack pulling at me and the wind tossing me around like a paper toy in a cyclone.

Time then had no meaning for me, only the gusts of wind marking the progress of my climb. When the wind died, I was able to climb easily; but when the wind gusted, I was unable to do anything but hold on.

All during the climb to the top I kept thinking about what this would be like under actual conditions with waves breaking around me, with the boat rolling and pitching in a heavy sea.

Given the right conditions I could be battered to death against the side of the ship. Not a very inviting thought. But neither was the thought of the strontium 90 that was possibly aboard the *Akai Maru,* bound for California.

TWO

Kuwait is halfway around the world from Washington, D.C., it's smaller than the state of New Jersey and it has less than one-third the population of Chicago. Yet it is one of the most important countries in the world.

Beneath the sands of the tiny desert sheikdom at the end of the Persian Gulf, lies one-fifth of the world's known oil reserves.

Paul Bridley, the public affairs officer for our embassy at Kuwait City, was waiting for me in customs hall of the ultramodern terminal building when I got off the TWA flight.

It was noon, local time, but my internal clock was still set on Washington time, which put me at three in the morning. I was dead tired and in no mood for any kind of games, but after only one look at Bridley I figured it was going to be a tough day.

He was short, had a round almost effeminate body and he was totally bald. When he spotted me coming through the doorway, he beamed and rushed across the room to me, his hand extended.

"Mr. Carter, welcome . . . welcome to Kuwait City," he bellowed. His voice boomed across the busy hall, and more than one person turned to look our way. "Paul Bridley, P.A. officer. Hope you had a good flight."

"I had a terrible flight, but thanks anyway," I said, keeping my voice low. What I didn't need was the attention of half the people in the airport.

"Well the chief is out of the country at the moment, but I'm sure Howard will make you feel welcome, perfectly welcome. It's not every day we get a new staffer out here. Sure can use you. Yes sir."

As Bridley continued to bellow at the top of his lungs, he took my arm and led me across the room to the customs officer at the end counter.

"Amail al-Mulwah al-Hafat, I'd like you to meet Nicholas Carter. He's been posted here to help us in the trade mission for awhile."

Al-Hafat smiled broadly, offered me a slight bow and then held out his hand for my passport. He barely glanced at the diplomatic visa which Hawk had arranged. He stamped the page and then returned it to me.

"Mr. Bridley tells me that you are an afficionado of *la disco*. I would like it very much for me and my younger wife to accompany you some evening." He looked over my shoulder. "Your wife, she will be joining you?"

"In a few weeks," I said, wondering what the hell Bridley had told the man and angry because he had drawn so much attention to me.

"Welcome to Kuwait then," al-Hafat said. "And please observe our laws."

"Thank you," I said, returning the man's slight bow. A few minutes later Bridley had retrieved my luggage from the diplomatic shipment, had tossed it carelessly into the back seat of a battered, gray

Chevrolet sedan, and we were heading away from the airport at a brisk pace.

"I don't know what the hell you were told, but what was all that glad-handing back there?" I snapped.

Bridley turned and glanced at me, his wide, stupid smile replaced with a lopsided grin, and he shrugged. "While in Rome do as the Romans expect you to do?" he offered.

"Meaning?" I asked.

"As long as you appear to be fat, dumb and happy it makes the Arabs feel superior. And if there's anything an Arab likes better than feeling superior, I've never discovered it. You'd be amazed at the doors opened to you if you're dumb."

"Strange talk for an embassy representative," I said, laughing.

"I didn't mean it that way," Bridley quickly protested. "What I meant to say is that Westerners have been giving the Arabs such a hard time for such a long time, that they appreciate feeling superior. I just oblige them, that's all."

"Thanks for the welcome anyway, and the ride," I said. "Do you know why I'm here?"

"Not really," Bridley remarked. "Except that it has something to do with the poor devil who showed up on our doorstep the other day. Radiation poisoning, from what I understand."

"Who else knows about it?" I asked.

Bridley glanced at me. "Knows about what? The deceased, your arrival or the connection?"

"All of it."

"The deceased—most of the embassy staff. Your arrival—ditto. The connection—damned few."

"Let's keep it that way."

"Fine by me, unless you start stirring things up," he said. Again he took his eyes off the road and glanced at me. "You *are* going to stir things up, aren't you."

"Probably," I said.

Bridley sighed almost theatrically. "Gone are the peaceful days."

We continued into town in silence for awhile, passing modernistic mosques in whose shadows were hovels. Overall, however, Kuwait City and its well-planned suburbs gave the impression of being spanking new and exceedingly clean. Only here and there was there evidence of poverty and of the nomadic existence these people had lived for thousands of years.

"I imagine you're going to need transportation while you're here," Bridley said a few minutes later. We had just come into the city proper through the port-and-customs area and I had been thinking about the cover story that Hawk had prepared for me.

As far as Bridley and the few others here in our embassy who knew I was coming were concerned, I was a special investigator for the Atomic Energy Commission, on loan to the State Department. Radioactive material had shown up here in the Mideast. It was my job to find out where it had come from. Nothing more.

"Yes," I answered him, coming out of my thoughts. "I'll need a driver as well. Someone I can trust."

"This is the car and I'm your driver," Bridley offered. "After all, if you can't trust your friendly P.A. officer, who can you trust . . . your banker?"

I laughed. "Have your people come up with an

identification on the dead man yet?"

"A possible ID," Bridley said. "Howard McQueen, our assistant deputy chief of mission has all the details for you. He wanted to be the one to brief you."

"A good guy or a bad guy?" I asked, instinctively liking and trusting Bridley despite his boisterousness.

"The dead man or McQueen?"

"McQueen," I said.

"He's an asshole, but what the hell, he's my boss and he is a loyal citizen of the U.S. of A."

"How are the Kuwait police being handled?"

"They don't know a thing," Bridley said. "We've got the body in the deep freeze."

"Literally?"

"Literally," he told me. "The corpse is hotter than a three dollar bill. One of our Marine guards who got close to him will probably develop leukemia before too long."

"That bad?"

"That bad," Bridley said. "As soon as the medics got a look at the body they isolated it, went through the standard drill and stuffed him in one of the freezers. Took eight guys half the afternoon to lug the thing out of the kitchen and into the maintenance garage."

"How about the Marine?"

"They sedated him and put him in isolation. McQueen wanted to wait for your arrival before he shipped him back to the States."

The U.S. Embassy is housed in a modernistic three-story complex of stone and glass, just off the

Beneid al-Gar. Its roofline bristles with communications equipment, and below, its expansive parking lot was full when Bridley pulled up at the main gate.

Four Marine guards immediately surrounded the car and checked mine as well as Bridley's identification papers. The efficiency I'm sure was more for my benefit than anything else. Since I was technically working for State, they'd want nothing but the best reports to get back home. I expected the entire embassy would be on alert status, even if they didn't know why I was here, until I left, but that was fine with me. It would make my job somewhat easier if I could get instant cooperation.

When we were finally allowed to pass, Bridley drove around to the back of the main building where he parked, then helped me with my two heavy suitcases—one of which contained the equipment Philips had prepared for me.

"Ninety-eight percent of our work is with big business—and I do mean big," Bridley said as we crossed under a covered walkway and he pulled out his keys to unlock a wide metal door. "One percent of the time we're dealing with tourists in trouble. The occasional woman who decides to go downtown in short shorts and a halter top and gets arrested. Or the occasional poor slob who runs out of money or has his passport stolen."

He had the door open and held it for me as I stepped inside, finding myself in a large vestibule, doors to the left and right, and an elevator straight ahead.

"And the last one percent?" I asked as Bridley made sure the door was firmly closed.

"Ever since Iran, we've been careful about physical security around here," he said. "The last one percent? This is it. The last time anything exciting happened around here was when a drunk Texan— worked for Aramco, I think—decided to shoot up one of the local watering holes. Found out he was ex-CIA. All hell broke loose for a few weeks."

He nodded toward the elevator and we crossed the room where he set my bag down and punched the call button. The indicator was on the third floor, but almost immediately it started down.

"The reason for the mini-briefing is McQueen," Bridley said. "He may be an ass, but he's been one hell of a shrewd businessman and a tough negotiator." He looked up at the elevator indicator again and then bent down and picked up my suitcase.

"I'm not here to negotiate a deal—" I started to say, but Bridley cut me off.

"We've got a possible incident going on here, Nick. McQueen wants more than assistant deputy chief of mission status. He wants to be an ambassador someday. He's a pal of Reagan's, and whenever possible he makes his points."

The elevator doors opened and we stepped inside. "Who knows," Bridley said as the door closed, "if he can make you out to look like a fool and yet still find out just where the poor slob who showed up dead came across the radioactive material, he'd be the hero."

I smiled. "Don't worry about it," I said. "But thanks for the warning."

The elevator bumped to a stop on the third floor, and as the doors slid open, Bridley winked at me. "Good luck," he said.

Howard McQueen's secretary told us that her

boss was waiting for me and we stowed my bags beside her desk.

"Is the other Marine guard still around?" I asked Bridley.

"Albion?" he said and nodded. "When you're done here, come over to my office, I'll have him there."

"Thanks," I said, and Bridley turned and waddled down the corridor as McQueen's secretary was announcing me over the intercom.

"You can go in now, Mr. Carter," the young woman said with a smile.

I returned her smile and then went into McQueen's office which was large, well-furnished and plushly carpeted. He was a tall, husky man with thick black hair, bushy eyebrows and large features. For just a moment I thought I was looking at the Soviet leader Brezhnev, but then the spell was broken as he came around his desk, his hand extended and a broad smile on his face.

"Welcome to Kuwait City, Mr. Carter," he said. He sounded Southern.

We shook hands, his grip iron hard, and he motioned me toward a chair.

"How is Washington these days?" he asked, going back behind his desk as I sat down.

"Hot," I said, "or at least I thought it was until I got here. It must be a hundred degrees outside."

"A hundred and eleven this afternoon. It's been warmer."

"Paul Bridley tells me that you have a possible ID on the dead man," I said. I wanted to get this over with as fast as possible and then find a nice cool room somewhere to sleep.

"That's right," McQueen said, somewhat irked.

He sat back in his chair. "I think your trip out here may have been a waste of time."

For just a moment the significance of his words did not sink in, but when they did, it was like a bombshell. I sat forward in my chair. "What?"

"I'll pass on a full report, of course. But your trip here was unnecessary as it turns out."

"I think you'd better explain yourself," I said, working hard to keep my voice even.

A momentary look of uncertainty crossed McQueen's features, but then he, too, sat forward and looked at his watch. "We should be hearing within the next few minutes," he said.

"Hearing what?" I asked, my heart beginning to accelerate.

"They can't get away. Our people have the place surrounded."

I jumped up from my chair and leaned way over the desk toward him. "What the hell have you done?"

"Listen here, I don't like your tone—" he started to protest, but I reached out and grabbed a handful of his shirt front and jerked him half out of his chair.

"My authority comes directly from the President," I snapped. "You can call him right now if you wish, but it would be the biggest mistake of your life."

"I—I," McQueen sputtered.

"What's going on here? Tell me now, before it's too late."

"Al-Mukhtar, Fahd al-Mukhtar. He's the dead man. Red Fist of November, we think. His girl-friend has been identified. She lives in Dasma."

"Your people are there now . . . at her apartment?"

"Yes," he squeaked.

"Where is it, exactly? The address?"

"Faisal Street. Number twenty-seven."

Low key and yet fast, Hawk had warned me before I left Washington. And unless I could beat McQueen's people to the apartment, the first of those instructions would be out the window.

I let go of McQueen, turned and raced across his office and out the door where I grabbed my two suitcases from beside the startled secretary's desk.

"Where's Bridley's office," I shouted.

"I—I," she stammered, and then she pointed down the corridor in the opposite direction from the elevator. "Three fifteen," she said.

McQueen was at his office door. "What do you think you're doing?" he screamed.

"Call your people off," I snapped over my shoulder, and then I was running down the corridor, two younger men jumping out of my way.

Bridley's office door was open and he was seated behind his desk facing a young man in a Marine uniform. They both looked up when I appeared in the doorway.

"Let's go, Bridley! *Now!*" I shouted.

Bridley got to his feet and came surprisingly fast around his desk, joining me in the corridor. McQueen was just coming toward us.

"I order you to come back here, Carter," he was screaming.

Bridley glanced at him and then at me. "Where are we going?"

"Twenty-seven Faisal Street, in Dasma," I said. "Do you know it?"

"It's about five minutes from here."

Several people had come out of their offices to see what all the commotion was about, and the young Marine guard who had been speaking with Bridley stepped out into the corridor as well.

"Bridley!" McQueen shouted, as we headed down the corridor toward the back stairs. "Soldier, stop those men!"

"I don't have my weapon, sir," the young Marine said, and then Bridley and I were in the stairwell hurrying down to the ground floor.

"McQueen is going to have a hemorrhage," Bridley said as we pounded down the stairs.

"He'll have more than that if we're not on time," I snapped.

Within a couple of minutes we had made it out the back door and piled into Bridley's old Chevy. He had the engine started, backed out of the parking slot with squealing tires, and we raced through the front gate past the bewildered Marine guards.

As Bridley drove, I quickly opened my suitcase that had been sent along with the diplomatic bags and retrieved my Luger, not bothering for the moment with my shoulder holster. When I had it loaded, I stuffed it in my belt and then opened the other suitcase from which I took the ultrasensitive Geiger counter that Philips had equipped me with.

Bridley had been watching all of this out of the corner of his eyes, as he hurried through town. Traffic was very light at this hour of the day, for which I was thankful.

"You *are* going to stir up trouble, aren't you," Bridley said.

"I'm trying my damndest to avoid it," I replied. "How much farther?"

"Just a couple of minutes."

We came around a traffic circle, the intersecting street marked in Arabic and English, FIRST

RING ROAD, and Bridley turned sharply to the right two blocks later.

"Dasma," he said, and he slowed down as he searched for Faisal Street.

We both spotted it at the same time, and a moment later we also both spotted the half a dozen military vehicles and two police units.

"Christ," I said, as Bridley pulled up and parked behind one of the jeeps.

I was out of the car before he had shut the engine off, and was racing down the blocked-off street toward a small crowd of people who had gathered to watch.

A Kuwaiti police officer held out his arm for me to stop and I was just about to stiff arm him out of the way, when Bridley raced up behind me and said something in Arabic to the man.

For a long second the policeman seemed to consider what Bridley had said to him, his hand resting on the butt of his holstered pistol, but then he nodded, stepped aside and let us pass.

We got to the front entrance of the apartment just as two men in Marine uniforms came stumbling out the door, shouting almost incoherently something about radiation and that it was too late.

Instantly they were surrounded by a half a dozen other Marines and several Kuwaiti police officers.

Bridley stepped into the middle of them, shoving a couple of the Marines aside. "What happened up there, John?" he shouted at one of the Marines who had come out of the building.

The young kid looked up at Bridley, his eyes wide, saliva running down from the corners of his mouth.

"John, what the hell happened?" Bridley shouted again.

"They're dead . . . second floor," the Marine stuttered. "Just like the first one. They're hot. Christ, I know they're hot."

"Bridley," I shouted, and the man turned my way. "Keep everyone out of the building. I'll be right back."

He nodded, less concerned about me, it seemed, than the young Marine. I turned and raced back to his car where I tore open the suitcase Philips had prepared for me and pulled out a fat plastic bag that contained the radiation suit.

In less than a minute I had the bag opened and had pulled the suit on over my street clothes, and then I hurried back to the crowd.

Bridley helped me pull the hood over my head and snap it to the shoulder fastenings, and then I pulled on the heavy gloves, picked up the Geiger counter and went into the building.

The narrow stairs were dirty and dark. I had to pick my way carefully to the second floor landing.

A door halfway down the narrow corridor was open, and as I headed for it, I flipped on the Geiger counter. Even through the heavy material of the hood I could hear the rapid clicking, the needle on the instrument's dial rapidly edging toward the red line.

At the doorway the clicking came much more rapidly and the needle hovered just at the red danger point.

Three people were in the tiny room. One of them a woman, the other two men. They were obviously dead and all of them were in as bad or worse shape than the man in the photographs Hawk had shown me.

Their hair was gone and their bodies were completely covered with wide, running sores.

I stepped carefully into the room, my stomach churning, and quickly searched the bodies, coming up with nothing but a few odd coins, a handkerchief and a comb.

The room was very small and was furnished with a broken-down couch on which the woman was sprawled, a couple of easy chairs, and in one corner a small refrigerator and a counter on which was a gas ring, a woman's purse lying beside it.

I moved carefully across the room, holding the Geiger counter out ahead of me. Everything was hot, including the purse.

Philips had given me a simple formula that would tell me how much time I could be safe while wearing the suit, at various radiation levels, but I couldn't think of it at the moment. I wasn't planning on remaining here much longer anyway.

I set the Geiger counter down on the cabinet and opened the woman's purse. Inside was some money, a set of keys, a few items of makeup and a letter. It was radioactive like everything else in the room and was written in Arabic, although the address and return address were in English.

It was addressed to Sheila Shabah al-Shabat, here at twenty-seven Faisal Street, Apartment 2-C, Kuwait. The return address was for a Hermil Zahle, in Beirut, Lebanon.

I stared at the name and return address for several long seconds, memorizing them, and then put the letter back in the purse. It would be too hot to take out of here.

Across the room from the kitchen area, was a closed door. I picked up the Geiger counter and headed across to it, but the needle suddenly went deep into the red, and at the door the clicking from the instrument was coming like an unmuffled motorboat engine.

Whatever was on the other side of the door had to be hot. Extremely hot.

For a moment I debated whether I should get the hell out of there right now or open the door. But I had to know if the beta canister was still here.

I stepped back a little way, balanced myself on one foot and kicked the door open. The Geiger counter went wild.

Five feet from the door, sitting next to the bed, was a squat metal canister laying on its side. The thick, lead-lined cover lay a few feet away.

On the outside of the container were the words: ISRAEL NUCLEAR ENERGY DIVISION, DEPT. OF ARMY, BEERSHEBA.

The canister was empty.

THREE

It took most of the rest of the afternoon for the embassy's medical team to clean up the mess on the street and then decontaminate my radiation suit so that I could get out of it.

The apartment building was evacuated and then sealed off, a much subdued McQueen promising the chief of Kuwait's police a full explanation within twenty-four hours.

A call had been placed immediately to Ambassador Leland Smith who was back in Washington; the entire situation was explained to him and then a U.S. Air Force nuclear decontamination team was dispatched from Ramstein, Germany to pick up the canister.

By the time Bridley and I finally left Dasma to return to the Embassy, I was dead tired. I had been on the go now, with little or no sleep, for more than seventy-two hours, and I wanted nothing more than to curl up in a corner somewhere and sleep. First, however, I was going to have to get a TWX off to Hawk, outlining the situation and asking authorization for my next step.

It was nearly seven o'clock P.M., by the time we had been cleared through the main gate, and

Bridley parked in his slot at the rear of the main complex.

He doused the car's headlights and shut off the engine; but instead of getting out he sat there, both hands on the steering wheel.

I had my door opened and was about to climb out when Bridley spoke to me, his voice raspy.

"Can you tell me what this is all about, Nick?"

I turned back. In the stray light from the perimeter fence and from the windows at the back of the main building, Bridley's face looked white, unhealthy. "What is it?" I asked. Something was wrong with the man.

An expression of deep anguish came into his eyes. "Neither of those Marines who went up to the apartment are going to make it," he said.

"McQueen will have to answer for them," I said. "It wasn't your fault. We did the best we could."

"McQueen *did* screw it up, didn't he?"

"What's wrong?" I asked gently. Bridley seemed to be on the verge of collapse. "Are you feeling all right?"

He nodded, but said nothing.

"Was one of those boys a friend of yours?"

"John—" he started to say, but the words were choked off. He turned away. "PFC John Bridley is my son."

"Christ," I said. "I'm sorry Paul." I wanted to say more to him, but there was nothing anyone could say that would help.

"If there are any others involved in this thing, catch them. Stop them."

"That's what I'm here for."

"I'd like to help," he said.

"I'll need the use of the embassy's communications room for a few hours, and then in the morning I'll probably need some transportation out to the airport."

"You're leaving?" he said sharply.

"Probably."

"But what about the people in the apartment, what about the others?"

"They won't be here in Kuwait. I've got a couple of leads."

He nodded. "He's only twenty-one," he said. Then he took a deep breath, let it out slowly, squared his shoulders and got out of the car.

We went back upstairs where I dumped my bags in his office, and then he took me down to the Communications Center in the basement, which was alive with traffic despite the lateness of the hour.

The entire embassy was on extra duty status in case any trouble developed over the incident in Dasma. The on-duty clerk told us that McQueen had been called over to the Kuwaitian Ministry of Defense a half an hour earlier, and that Ambassador Smith was already on his way back. It was going to take a long time for the dust to settle here in Kuwait, but in the meantime I had a job to do that had been made doubly difficult by McQueen's rash move.

The communications officer was a young man with long hair, flowing mustache and was dressed in an unpressed denim suit. He seemed harried.

"Stewart Gillingham, chief of communications, Nick Carter," Bridley introduced us. "Nick is on special status from State, and is cleared for the top. He'll be needing a clear channel tonight. Give him whatever he asks for."

"Yes sir," Gillingham said, although I could see that he did not like it.

"Why don't you go home and get a few hours sleep," I told Bridley. "I won't be needing anything until morning."

Bridley shook his head. "I'm going to have to stick around for a few hours anyway," he said. "So when you're done down here come on up to my office. I've got a bottle of twelve-year-old Scotch that needs opening."

"I may be several hours," I told him.

Bridley shrugged. "That's all right. It's a big bottle," he said, and he turned and waddled back to the elevator.

"Now," Gillingham said, "it's kind of jumping around here at the moment. If you'll tell me exactly what you need, Mr. Carter, I'll get it for you, and then I can return to my work."

"Have you got a secure channel with State?" I asked.

The man's eyebrows rose. "Only one," he said. "And it'll be jammed with triple A cats until sometime tomorrow afternoon."

"I'm going to commandeer it for a few hours," I said. Gillingham started to protest but I held him off. "It'll save us both a lot of time and headaches if you'll just cooperate with me for a couple of hours. By morning I'll be gone."

Something flashed in Gillingham's eyes, but then he sighed and smiled. "Is that a promise?"

I laughed. "A promise."

"The shop is all yours. What do you need?"

"A one-time cipher book and someplace secure to work."

"The channel is encrypted—" Gillingham

started to say, but again I cut him off.

"I know. But I'll still need the cipher book and a place to work."

"All right," he said. "Secret or top secret?"

He was about to get a shock. "Presidential," I said softly.

He opened his mouth to say something, but then shut it. He was impressed. There were only a dozen people in the world who had access to such a cipher book. A copy was kept at each embassy around the world, but it was only used during extreme emergencies—and only by a handful of people.

"I'll need the alpha-numeric sequence from you," he said.

"Dig out the book and I'll sign the form."

He showed me across the large room that was filled with teletype and facsimile machines to a small office that contained a cluttered desk and a half a dozen file cabinets. "Make yourself at home," he offered. "I'll get the book."

When he was gone I sat down at the desk, took off my coat and loosened my tie. I pulled a large pad of paper forward, grabbed a pencil from a holder and started to work.

Gillingham was back a few minutes later, carrying the bulky cipher book that was sealed in a padded envelope.

I took the authorization form from him and quickly filled in the proper twenty-seven unit alpha-numeric code, then handed it back.

He checked it against a covered list on the outside of the envelope, countersigned the authorization and handed the book to me. "First time I've ever dealt with one of these," he said.

"No one is to come in here under any circumstances until I'm finished. Do you understand?" I said.

"Yes sir," Gillingham answered, and he left, closing the door firmly behind him.

Sleep, I thought, before I began. Just a little while longer.

It took me the better part of two hours to first write out my message to Hawk in plain language and then encode it from the Presidential cipher group book.

I wrote a fairly concise account of what had happened here in Kuwait, including the fact that I had found an empty beta canister with Israeli markings in the apartment.

At least I had accomplished one of my goals: finding out where the nuclear material had come from. We had long suspected the Israelis of having nuclear capabilities, now this proved it.

How the beta canister had been taken from the nuclear facility at Beersheba, however, and transported here to Kuwait was another problem that would have to wait until I received a reply.

In the message, I also told Hawk about the letter I had found in the woman's purse and asked for Navy help to get me into Beirut. Before I attempted to board the *Akai Maru* at sea, I wanted to know if anyone else involved in the project was still alive.

Getting aboard the ship was going to be difficult enough; I didn't relish the idea of trying it if someone aboard was expecting me.

When I was finished, I resealed the book in the padded envelope and brought it, as well as my bulky message, out to Gillingham. The addressee number I had written at the top of the first page was a blind number at the State Department in Washington. When the message arrived there, day or night, it would be automatically shunted to Hawk's office on Dupont Circle.

"I want this sent out immediately," I told Gillingham. "I'll wait for the reply."

"How about the book?"

"Lock it up," I said. "I'm going to catch a couple hours of sleep, and it's not the kind of thing I want laying around."

"I'll bring it back with the reply," Gillingham said.

I turned and went back into the office where I closed the door, sat down at the desk and put my feet up. I suppose I was asleep before the chair had rocked all the way back, and I suppose I dreamed, although I wasn't aware of a thing until Gillingham was standing over me shaking my shoulder.

"Mr. Carter . . . Mr. Carter . . ."

I opened my eyes, blinked and then dropped my feet from the desk top. "What's the matter," I mumbled. "Something wrong with the channel?"

"It's two in the morning," he told me. "You've been asleep since around ten. Your reply has come in."

It took my fuzzy brain a moment to register what he had just said to me, but when it did I took a deep breath and let it out slowly.

He handed the cipher group book to me, along with a single page of copy.

"This is all?" I asked.

"That's it," he said. "I'd like to release the line for traffic now, if I may."

"Thanks, I'm through with it," I said absently,

and Gillingham turned and left the office.

It took me less than half an hour to decode the brief message Hawk had sent me, and it held no surprises.

WE SUSPECTED BEERSHEBA IN-STALLATION STOP PRESIDENT HAS BEEN ADVISED THIS AFTERNOON STOP MEET USN CMDR ROBERT JOR-DAN, TERMINAL HELLENIKON AIR-PORT, ATHENS SOONEST STOP CARE-FUL IN BEIRUT BUT SPEED ESSEN-TIAL NOW STOP.
ENDOFMESSAGE
HAWK

After I had shredded the message as well as my scratch pad, I returned the cipher group book to Gillingham, thanked him for his help and headed upstairs to Bridley's office. I was going to have to take the first possible flight out of here in the morning and Bridley would have to arrange the shipment of my bags to Athens under diplomatic immunity.

It would have been much simpler for me if I could have taken a commercial flight to Beirut. But that would be impossible. Besides the fact that I did not want to announce my presence in Lebanon so openly, the country was still at war—the Southern Christian forces battling with the Moslems who held the capital city.

Under the best of circumstances Beirut would be an unhealthy place for me to be. I didn't want to make it any worse.

Upstairs, the embassy was just as busy as the communications center had been, the junior staffers worrying through reports and counter reports, the senior staffers sweating out short range, medium range and long range assessments. All hell was going to break loose when Ambassador Smith returned and everyone wanted to be as well prepared as possible.

No one answered when I knocked on Bridley's door, but I stepped inside anyway. The overhead light was off, the only illumination in the room coming through the window from outside.

Bridley was alone, seated behind his desk, his back to the door, staring out the window. A nearly finished quart of Chivas Regal was on the desk.

"Paul?" I said softly.

"Are you finished downstairs?" he asked without turning around. He did not sound drunk.

"Yes. But I'm going to need a little help getting out of here in the morning."

He turned around, put the glass he had been holding down on the desk and flipped on the lamp. His eyes were red rimmed and puffy, but whether it was from too much liquor, lack of sleep or something else, I didn't know. Nor would I ask.

"I just got back," he said looking up at me. "They're shipping John back to the States the day after tomorrow. He's down in the dispensary, pretty heavily sedated."

"Listen," I said. "Someone else can make the travel arrangements for me—"

Bridley cut me off. "It's my job," he said. "Where are you headed?"

"Athens," I said. "I have to be there as soon as possible."

"Flight leaves at seven in the morning. Cairo direct. We can get you a connecting flight from there with no problems. I'll transship your luggage with you under a diplomatic seal."

"No military aircraft in the area?" I asked on an off chance.

Bridley smiled wryly. "None that we'd care to admit. But it depends upon how flashy you want to be."

"Low key," I said. "The commercial flight will be fine."

He looked at me for a long moment. "Won't be anyone out there until around six." He looked at his watch. "Which gives us a couple of hours, or so. Care for a drink?"

"Sure," I said, and I sat down as he pulled another glass from a desk drawer and poured it half full.

"Cheers," he said.

It took nearly four hours to fly from Kuwait to Cairo, where I had a forty-five minute layover, and another two-and-a-half hours to Athens. I did manage to catch a couple of hours sleep through all of that, so that by the time we touched down at Hellenikon Airport, I was reasonably alert.

Navy Commander Bob Jordan was waiting for me on the opposite side of VIP customs, and I was sure by the expression on his face that he recognized me. But he was cautious.

"Nick Carter?" he asked softly, as he approached.

I nodded. "You must be Jordan."

"What's your girlfriend's name?"

I looked at him for a long moment, wondering

just what the hell Hawk had told him. "Which one?"

Jordan seemed surprised. "Japan?" he said. "Kazuka."

He smiled, relief evident in his expression, and he took my suitcases. "I was told to be careful."

"I don't think I'd care to have my love life the subject of a Navy file," I said as we headed across the terminal toward the front doors.

Jordan laughed. "Your secret is safe with me."

A plain gray Navy staff car was waiting for us out front. Jordan put my suitcases in the front seat next to the driver, and he and I piled in the back.

A second later we were heading away from the terminal toward the military side of the airport.

"What have you got on line for me?" I asked.

"We've got an SH-3A Sea King helicopter standing by to take you out to the *Whiteshark*. She's a Kennedy-class nuke submarine."

"Never heard of her," I said.

Jordan didn't reply, and I didn't press.

"Captain Newton Farmington is expecting you."

"Where is the ship located at this moment?" I asked.

"About a hundred miles out."

"Any Russians in the vicinity?" I asked.

Jordan looked at me. "Newt has your orders. I'm just the delivery boy."

"I see," I said. But I wanted to cover myself all the way into Beirut. The less that was known about my whereabouts, or about anything suspicious happening in the vicinity, the better I would feel. Hawk did not like it when his people pulled rank in the field, but I had no other choice. "I don't know what kind of strings you pull, commander, but before I get aboard that helicopter you're going to have to find out for me if the *Whiteshark* has a Russian shadow."

Jordan's smile was gone. "I don't know what strings *you* pull, Mr. Carter, but I do have my orders."

"You don't want to find out what strings I pull," I told him sharply. I was still overtired. "But I'm sure your orders specified *full* cooperation."

Jordan nodded. "They did."

"Fine," I said, "then we understand each other." I pulled out a cigarette and lit it.

We made it to the military hangar across from the civilian terminal. Once inside, the driver stowed my bags in the back of the Sikorsky helicopter, while Jordan hurried up to the operations room.

He was gone less than five minutes, and when he returned he seemed grim-lipped. Someone up the line must have chewed him out. "It's clear," he said. "The nearest Soviet vessel is a trawler about five-hundred miles off."

"Thanks for the lift and the information," I said. I turned and climbed up through the side door of the helicopter. The pilot looked back at me and when I was strapped in, he gave me the thumbs-up sign with a questioning look on his face.

Beside me on the bulkhead was a headset which I pulled on. Immediately the pilot's voice came to me.

"Is there a problem, sir?" he asked.

"There may be," I said. Jordan stood off to the side looking at me through the still open door. "There's a Russian trawler about five-hundred miles off the *Whiteshark*. I want to avoid radar detection. Can you do it?"

"Yes sir," the pilot said. "But we're going to have to come in pretty low. It could be bumpy and a bit hairy."

"Whatever it takes, I don't want them to know we've approached the sub."

"Yes sir," the pilot said, and I pulled the headset off, sat back and closed my eyes.

FOUR

"MR. CARTER TO THE BRIDGE. MR. CARTER TO THE BRIDGE," the speaker over the desk in my tiny cabin blared.

I jumped up from my bunk, crossed the room and hit the call button. "On my way," I said, releasing the switch.

It was a few minutes after two in the morning according to my watch. I had been lowered from the helicopter to the deck of the submarine about four yesterday afternoon, had been immediately hustled below, and then we submerged.

The helicopter pilot had been damned good, and as far as our surveillance radar detectors had been able to determine, the Soviet trawler had not picked us up.

Only ten hours had elapsed since that time, so I was reasonably certain that we had not crossed half the length of the Mediterranean to the coast of Lebanon, not unless the *Whiteshark* was capable of underwater speeds in excess of sixty-miles-per-hour.

Captain Newton Farmington had turned out to be exactly the opposite of Commander Jordan in every way. Where Jordan was tall and somewhat on the husky side, Farmington was short and thin. Where Jordan was the jolly sort, Farmington was tight-mouthed, a permanent scowl on his face. But he was competent and his men had a great respect for him.

I dressed quickly, splashed some cold water on my face and made my way forward to the bridge where Farmington was waiting for me at the periscope head.

"Over here Mr. Carter. I want you to look at something," he snapped.

There were several other officers on the bridge and all of them were watching me out of the corner of their eyes. I supposed it was because civilians were not often guests aboard naval warships.

Farmington stepped aside and I leaned forward, placing my forehead on the cushioned periscope rest, and a second later, when my eyes were adjusted to the night sight optics, I was able to pick out what appeared to be a large harbor and a city beyond it in a semicircular bay. From time to time I could see what appeared to be explosions, and at several spots within the city fires were clearly visible.

For several long moments I wracked my brain trying to figure out where we were, what the fighting was all about and why the captain had interrupted this mission. But then it struck me that I was looking at Beirut less than two-thousand yards away.

I straightened up and looked at Farmington. "When did we arrive?"

The captain almost smiled. "About two hours ago."

The shock must have shown on my face, because

he quickly added: "That means this boat is capable of some rather high speeds."

"Eighty-miles-an-hour, maybe?" I asked. I was impressed. "I had no idea our Navy—or any navy for that matter—had anything quite so sophisticated."

"That, Mr. Carter, is a highly classified bit of information. I want you to remember it."

"So is this mission, captain," I said dryly, and I turned back to the scope. Fighting was definitely going on in the city, which would in some respects make my job a bit easier. No one would be looking for me. "What is the local time?" I asked.

"Oh-three-ten hours," Farmington said.

I straightened up again and stepped away from the periscope. "The mission starts now," I said. I had seen a tangle of wreckage at the south end of the harbor that would provide me with a fine cover. "I want a rubber raft and a set of dark coveralls, plus a night kit."

"You're going ashore into that?" the captain asked.

I nodded. "I have a job to do."

"Indeed," he said, and he turned and barked out several orders to his executive officer, and the man in turn quickly got on the ship's intercom.

"I'll also need some kind of signalling unit for our rendezvous," I added.

"How long do you expect to be ashore?"

I thought a moment. "It'll probably take forty-five minutes to actually get ashore. With luck I'll need a couple of hours in the city, and another forty-five minutes to get back out."

"Dawn," the captain said. "You'll be cutting it very close." He turned to the first radio officer.

"Install an HB-73 in the raft."

"Yes sir," the man snapped.

"We'll equip you with a VHF transmitter. When you start back out, key it twice, three times, twice. We'll come in for you."

"Where will you be?"

"A few miles out, just off the continental slope."

"Fine," I said and I turned to go back to my cabin to get my weapons and the Geiger counter, but Farmington stopped me.

"One last thing, Mr. Carter," he said.

I turned back and waited for him to continue.

"This boat cannot be compromised. That's a direct Presidential order. If you get yourself into too much trouble, we won't be able to do very much for you."

"Of course," I said, and I left the bridge.

* * * *

I was in my skivvies, my shoulder holster over my T-shirt and my stiletto strapped to my forearm, when a young seaman came to my quarters with a pair of soft-soled boots, a black, Navy commando coverall suit, a black knit cap and a night kit that included thin leather gloves, a black haversack and dark grease paint.

When he saw my weapons his eyes widened. "Here are the things you wanted, sir," he said.

I took them from him, but before he left he looked again at the stiletto.

"Are you really going ashore this evening, sir?" he asked.

I smiled. "That's right."

"Good luck then, sir."

"Thanks," I said. "I have a hunch I'm going to need it."

Five minutes later I was dressed, had blackened my face with the grease paint, had stuffed the Geiger counter in the haversack and had gone forward to the bow hatch where the executive officer and two of his men were waiting. One of them was dressed in the same gear as I was.

"What's going on?" I asked softly. The boat was quiet here and the only illumination came from a low-wattage red light overhead.

"The captain suggested we send one of our people with you to act as a backup."

I shook my head. "Thank the captain for me, but I'm doing this alone."

The executive officer seemed ready to argue, but then thought better of it. "As you wish, sir," he said. "Are you ready to go?"

I nodded, and he reached up and hit the intercom button. "Ready forward," he said.

A moment later I could hear the air tanks purging the ballast water, and the deck tilted upward. For several long seconds we all watched the indicator lights on the hatch above our heads, until the red light winked off and the amber light came on.

The executive officer nodded, and one of the men scrambled up the ladder, spun the hatch wheel and shoved the hatch open. A small spray of water shot down on us, and a moment later the pungent odor of seawater mixed with the sour smell of tidal flats wafted in.

The second man scrambled up the ladder, the executive officer wished me luck and I climbed topside.

The submarine's deck was barely afloat and each small wave in the sheltered bay sent water rushing across our feet.

Aft, the black conning tower rose a long way out of the water, but it would be nearly invisible from the shore even if someone was watching for it.

It took less than thirty seconds for the two men to break out a small rubber raft from an underwater locker, inflate it and toss it into the water after first placing the small transmitter in one of its side pockets.

Even from here I could hear the sound of gunfire and smell the acrid odor of smoke from fires within the city. As long as I wasn't spotted by a sniper or discovered by a patrol from either side, the fighting would act as a perfect cover.

I climbed down into the rubber raft, snapped the plastic oars in their locks and released the tether line.

Before I had gotten ten yards away, the water rose up around me in a gentle swell, and when I looked back the submarine was gone, only a few ripples showing where it had been.

The sea breeze was at my back and the tide was evidently running in, because I made it past the half-submerged wreckage of two cargo ships and ashore in something under thirty-five minutes.

The fighting was to my north, closer to the center of the city, but as I pulled the rubber raft beneath the planking of a large wooden cargo dock and tied it to one of the pilings, I was careful just the same not to make any noise.

The structure supporting the dock was much like a railroad trestle, so I was easily able to climb up the cross beams and from there make my way to the edge. For several long seconds I held my breath, straining with every sense to detect any noises above. But there was nothing other than the sporadic gunfire in the distance.

I peered over the top careful to make each movement slow and very deliberate. There were a few crates stacked to my left; to the right, parked near the warehouse, was a dilapidated forklift truck with both its front tires missing.

The entire dock area was in darkness and appeared to be deserted, so after a few moments I climbed on top, and keeping low, raced across to the deeper shadow alongside the building.

I had been in Beirut on other assignments before, but the city had always been bright and alive, the people mostly prosperous looking and happy. Now, however, the city was dark, with an evacuated air to it, the only noise and light coming from the fighting going on in the downtown section.

I had studied a detailed street map of the city from the submarine's charts and had pinpointed the address from the envelope in the dead woman's purse back in Kuwait City.

The number was in Basta, which was a Sunni Muslim slum district in the southeast quarter of the city. From where I stood it was less than two miles away. The only trouble was that it was in the same direction the fighting was coming from.

I lowered the zipper on the front of my dark coveralls a couple of inches to allow myself easier access to Wilhelmina, my Luger, loosened the snaps on the cuffs of my sleeves as well, and then started away from the dock along a narrow alleyway between the warehouses.

As I ran, up on the balls of my feet so that I made absolutely no noise, all my senses were alert. To be caught here like this would mean instant death. No arrest, no interrogation and no trial, just a bullet in the head.

I had made my way out of the warehouse district in less than five minutes and was hurrying along a dark street, when I ran into a patrol and was forced into ducking behind a pile of foul-smelling garbage that had been left at the curb.

A half a dozen soldiers in Muslim robes, each carrying a long desert rifle, trotted down the middle of the street, and as they passed my hiding place I could hear their heavy breathing and an occasional grunt.

I waited a full sixty seconds after they had passed before I slipped from my hiding place and continued toward Basta. The closer I got to the slum district, the more garbage was laying rotting in the streets and the more ramshackle the buildings became.

Hermil Zahle lived at fifty-two Rasheiya Place, which despite its high-sounding name was nothing more than an extremely narrow cul de sac off a wider avenue. The buildings here looked as if they were ready to topple over at any second, and most of the windows had been broken with only a few boarded over.

The fighting was much closer now, no more than a couple of blocks farther toward the heart of the city. From where I stood in the doorway of what once had been a shop of some sort, I could see the tops of several large, modern office buildings, half destroyed, over the roofline across the street.

I don't know how many times I have nearly lost

my life or how often my instinct for survival has saved it, but at this moment I had the very strong feeling that something was drastically wrong.

Farther down the wide avenue were the wreckages of three automobiles, at least one of them a late model American car. Chunks of concrete, metal and glass littered the roadway, and twenty yards from where I stood I could see a fairly large pile of brass shell casings. Some intense fighting had gone on here, probably recently.

I turned back to look down the dark cul de sac; number fifty-two was at the end of the opening in the buildings. As I studied the roofline and the windows, and tried to penetrate the dark shadows near the street level, the feeling that I was walking into a trap became even stronger inside me.

I held my breath for a long time, straining to hear something, anything over the sounds of the fighting going on a couple of blocks away. And then I heard it.

It was a high-pitched, keening sound. At first I thought it was a cat mewing, or perhaps a dog, weak with pain, crying. But a few moments later I heard the distinct word, "Please," from the darkness. It had come from the end of the cul de sac.

The return address on the envelope was for an apartment on the third floor. All the buildings in the cul de sac were three stories tall.

Checking the main avenue once more to make sure no one was coming, I turned away from the doorway, crunched over some glass and stepped through the broken display window of the shop and into the dark interior.

Something skittered away from me to the left

and I pulled out my Luger, levered a round into the chamber and had the safety off, even before I realized it had probably been nothing more than a rat.

For several long seconds I stood there, my heart racing, my finger tight on the trigger, but then I relaxed and went farther inside.

The dim light from a fire down the block provided the only illumination inside the shop, which had been completely stripped, but it only took me a few seconds to find a back door that opened onto a narrow, open stairway.

Thirty feet above was a broken skylight which provided enough illumination for me to quickly make my way upstairs, and then to the roof through a thin steel door.

From here the sounds of the battle raging at the city's center were much louder, and although other large buildings farther up the block obstructed my view, I could see the flashes from automatic weapons to the northwest, and fires seemed to be raging everywhere.

The roofline between where I stood and the end of the cul de sac, about seventy-five yards away, was irregular, with slanted dormers, some areas of slate tiles, others of tar and gravel and still others of tin.

It looked very much like the roofline of any slum in Paris, which was not entirely surprising because for a time before the end of World War II the city had been controlled by the French and British.

I was about to start forward, when I noticed a point of light about ten yards to my right, and I froze, not moving a muscle.

For several long seconds I wondered if I had

been imagining things, but then I saw the point of light again. This time it moved upward in a short arc, glowed brightly for a moment and then died.

It was a cigarette. Someone was here on the roof smoking a cigarette.

Carefully I crouched down, then slowly swiveled to the right, and moved around toward the back of the line figure that was standing behind a squat chimney.

As I silently worked my way around him, I holstered my Luger and withdrew my stiletto, careful with each step to make sure I made absolutely no noise.

Now on the other side of the chimney I was downwind from the man, and I could smell the harsh scent of the cheap cigarette he was smoking as well as the strong odor of sweat.

Very slowly I moved around the edge of the chimney, and then bending down I picked up a small stone and tossed it out into the middle of the roof where it landed with a soft, almost inaudible clatter.

I could hear the man suck in his breath, the cigarette arched out in front of me, and then a man in black Muslim robes, armed with a submachine gun, stepped around the chimney, his back to me.

"*Hai*," I said softly, and he turned around, the machine gun coming my way, as my right arm slammed upward, burying the stiletto to the haft in his throat.

I jerked my wrist sharply to the left, and the man was down with barely a grunt, blood spurting everywhere at first, then dying down to nothing as the man's heart stopped beating.

I dropped to one knee beside the guard to make

sure he was dead, then wiped the stiletto on his
robes and replaced it in its chamois sheath. I
searched his body, coming up with a Lebanese
Army Night Fighters Unit metal identification
disc, as well as an envelope containing one thousand Lebanese pounds.

What in hell was he doing with that kind of money? It didn't make sense.

For a long moment I knelt there trying to figure
it out, but then I finally pocketed the envelope with
the money and the man's identification disc. I had
no idea what I was going to run into, but I wanted
some kind of a backup, something that would give
me at least a slight delay if I was stopped and chal-
lenged.

I made it the rest of the way over the roofs to the
end of the cul de sac, where I searched for and
finally found a half-rotted wooden trapdoor which
I eased open.

Below was some kind of an inner vestibule landing with stairs spiraling down the middle of it and
four doors, one on each side, opening from it.

There was absolutely no noise from within, and
only a very dim light from a pair of skylights on the
other side of the vestibule from the trapdoor.

I listened for a long time at the opening, but
could hear nothing from below; so I finally lowered
myself through, dropping down as quietly as I
could, remaining for a second or two in a half
crouch where I landed.

No alarm was sounded, no one came out to investigate, and after a while I straightened up. The
place reeked of some rotting smell which I couldn't
define, but it made my stomach rumble.

I quickly opened the haversack and withdrew the

Geiger counter and flipped it on. The needle remained at the calibrated zero point, with only an occasional click from the tiny speaker, which Philips had explained to me came from normal background radiation.

I held the unit out in front of me and slowly swung it around in a complete circle, pointing it at each of the unnumbered apartment doors. But still there was nothing.

Whatever Hermil Zahle's connection with the woman in the apartment back in Kuwait City was, it did not apparently include the handling of the strontium 90.

I stuffed the Geiger counter back in the haversack, pulled out my Luger and had started toward one of the apartment doors, when the door to my right swung open as I swiveled around.

A large man dressed in a plain gray suit stood there, an automatic of some kind in his hand. For a split second we looked at each other, and then he started to raise his gun.

I fired twice, the noise in the narrow vestibule deafening, the first shot hitting him in the chest and the second in his face, sending him crashing backward into the apartment.

Someone started up the stairs as I raced across the vestibule, leaped over the dead man's body and entered the tiny apartment.

A moment later someone called from the corridor, "Viktor! Viktor!"

I spun around and from the open door caught a movement at the center of the vestibule as a man's head and shoulders appeared from the stairwell.

He turned at the last moment and spotting me, started to fall back as I raised the Luger. I fired once, hitting him squarely in the forehead.

Whoever they were, I had just run out of time. It would only be a matter of a minute or two at the most before the place would be crawling with Muslim military units.

Quickly I bent down, flipped open the dead man's coat at my feet and extracted his wallet. Inside was a standard Soviet Embassy identification card. KGB.

Suddenly the Muslim soldier on the rooftop with the thousand Lebanese pounds was made clear. He had been paid to act as a lookout.

I turned and went all the way inside the apartment. The living room was a mess, the couch overturned, the stuffing out of it, the wallpaper ripped off, the plaster beneath it gouged out. In the bedroom were a man and a woman, both nude and both very much dead.

They had been brutally tortured, and at the end their wrists had been slit, evidently to make sure that they could watch themselves bleed to death.

The KGB. The single thought kept running through my brain.

I turned away from the bedroom, hurried back to the body by the door and, this time, searched all the pockets. If he was on his way out, he might have found what he had come looking for.

I found a manila envelope in one of his large coat pockets. Quickly I tore it open and from inside extracted a half a dozen documents that at first glance looked like military passes.

Holding them toward the light coming from the skylight overhead, I immediately recognized them. Israeli Military installation passes. Beersheba Nuclear Depot.

It explained how the beta canister had been taken from the Israelis. But the only reason the KGB would be interested in these passes, was if they had supplied them.

This had been a Soviet plot all along. But what were they trying to do? What could they possibly accomplish by stealing strontium 90, removing it from its protective canister and then presumably placing it aboard the *Akai Maru?* It just did not make any sense.

What sounded like two trucks screeched to a halt outside, and a moment later I could hear the shouts of at least a dozen soldiers down on the street.

I stuffed the Israeli documents in the pocket of my coveralls, jumped over the body, and in the vestibule landing looked over the rail of the stairwell just as the ground floor door burst open. At least a dozen soldiers, all wearing the Christian Forces uniform, started up the stairs.

Stuffing my Luger in its holster, I climbed up on the stairwell rail, and balancing there managed to leap high enough so that I was just able to catch the edge of the trapdoor opening with my fingertips.

For a long, agonizing moment I held there, slipping backward, but then I managed to force my left hand farther over the edge of the raised lip, and finally pulled myself all the way through.

I just managed to close the trapdoor and scramble silently to one of the cracked, dirty skylights, when the soldiers burst from the stairwell on the third floor and pulled the body of the KGB agent from the doorway of the apartment.

Several of them went inside, and a few seconds later they were back.

With any luck they would be occupied with the

belief that for some reason the two agents had had a shootout, killing each other, and would not suspect a third party. *With any luck.*

I turned and hurried across the roof to the open metal door that led down to the shop on the main avenue, and a couple of minutes later I had made it downstairs, had slipped outside and was racing south to my rubber raft.

FIVE

For several long, agonizing moments I hid in the shadows by the warehouse, watching the six Muslim soldiers fifty yards away pulling my rubber raft up from beneath the docks.

Most likely I had been spotted coming in from farther up the shoreline, but by the time they had managed to dispatch troops to intercept me I had landed and had made it away from the dock.

But now they had my only means of communicating with the submarine.

For an instant I debated with myself whether or not I could take them all out. But I dismissed the idea. I was an accurate shot with a Luger, even over these distances, but it would be impossible to kill six soldiers and then get away. Even if all the luck was with me, it would be impossible.

They found the radio and after one of them had examined it for a moment, he threw it down savagely and smashed it with his boot heel, while two of the others put several long slits in the rubber raft with their bayonets.

Even from here the hissing noise of the escaping gas was loud, and behind me, back toward the heart of the city the fighting continued to rage.

I really had only one option left, I figured, standing there watching the soldiers destroy my planned means of escape. And that was finding another boat, getting a few miles off shore and somehow attracting the attention of the submarine before the dawn came, making it impossible for them to surface.

The airport was too far to the east for me to reach on foot, and even if I did make it that far, there would be no guarantee I would find an airplane I could fly that was in working order.

Going overland, south to the Israeli border, would be even more impossible. Besides having to pass through the Muslim as well as the Southern Christian lines, I would somehow have to slip unnoticed past the Israelis who would shoot at anything coming their way from Lebanon.

It was going to have to be a boat. I turned and, keeping to the shadows, edged away from the dock until I figured I was far enough away from the soldiers to make an all-out dash for it. Then, I headed in a dead run down a narrow street that roughly paralleled the waterfront.

As I ran, the sounds of the fighting became louder and louder, and the narrow alley seemed to angle farther away from the bay.

Three blocks away the alley made an abrupt turn to the left, immediately opening onto a wide avenue that was blocked off by piles of sandbags. At least a hundred Southern Christian soldiers had taken up positions behind the sandbags, evidently waiting for the battle to come that way.

Too late I realized what I had stumbled into. Although I had only been exposed to view for a brief instant before I fell back, a half a dozen automatic rifles opened fire, the bullets ricocheting and whining off the pavement and the brick buildings around me.

I turned and started back down the alley when the lights of a vehicle stabbed the darkness ahead. The engine was grinding at high speed. I was trapped.

Dropping to one knee I pulled out Wilhelmina, my Luger, and steadying it with both hands, I fired three quick rounds at the headlights, one of them going out, and a moment later the other swerved crazily to the left. The vehicle crashed into one of the buildings.

I yanked the haversack off my shoulder, turned, and swinging it overhead like a sling, threw it toward the wide avenue.

"Bomb! Bomb! Bomb!" I shouted, and I leaped to the left, crashing head first through a store window, protecting my face and neck at the last instant with my arms.

I fell onto something soft, rolled over twice and jumped to my feet.

Outside there were the sounds of several men shouting out orders, and as I backed farther into the dark room, the window frame and part of the plaster wall to my right exploded under the concentrated fire of at least two heavy caliber machine guns.

I turned and immediately stumbled through a beaded doorway into a small hallway from which a set of stairs led up. Without hesitation I hurried up, my Luger in hand, trying to make as little noise as I possibly could.

It would not take the military unit outside very long to figure out that I would try for the roof, and cut that means of escape off. If that happened I would be dead for sure, although if I had stopped at that moment to think, I would not have given myself very high odds for survival in any case.

On the second floor the stairs ended in a narrow, low-ceilinged corridor that snaked and twisted into the darkness to my left. Downstairs the soldiers were battering the door down, which left me absolutely no choice. I felt like a rat in a maze that was being flooded behind me.

I left the landing and plunged into the dark corridor, bumping off the walls as they twisted right and left, and more than once banged my head on low beams as I groped my way forward.

After a few minutes I began to realize that all the buildings along the alleyway, through which I had come from the dock, were interconnected by this narrow passageway, and I began to have a real hope that I'd find a way out of this after all.

The hope lasted only a few seconds, however, when I came up against a blank, bricked-over wall. The end of the corridor.

For several long seconds I felt along the wall, floor to ceiling, for any kind of an opening—but there was none.

Behind me, but still a long way off, I could hear the sounds of the soldiers coming. They would be cautious for a little while longer, not knowing what to expect from me. But to be caught here like this, in some godforsaken, war-torn city. . .

The thought was too much. I flipped Wilhelmina's safety off and charged down the corridor, back the way I had come, my left hand out, the fingertips brushing against the wall to help guide me.

About twenty feet back from the brick dead end, I passed a small wooden door and pulled up short. The soldiers were much closer now and it would only be a matter of seconds before they were on me, so I backed up a few feet and charged the door with my shoulder.

The wood splintered easily and the door flung inward to a small apartment. An old man and a woman sat huddled on a bed in one corner, the only light in the room from a candle on the table next to them. Directly across from the door was a window, the ragged curtains moving slightly in a light breeze.

I leaped across the room, tore the curtains aside and lifted the window that opened onto a fully enclosed ventilation shaft.

The soldiers were just down the corridor now. As I stuck my head out the window and looked up, I saw that the edge of the roof was only a few feet overhead, so I stuffed the Luger back into its holster, climbed out the window, and holding onto the frame for balance, I reached up with my right hand, my fingers finding and curling around the lip of a drain gutter.

A moment later I had a grip on the gutter with my left hand and I pulled myself up and over onto the roof.

I rolled over twice away from the edge, scrambled to my feet and raced away. Seconds later the roof behind me was ripped with automatic fire from below in the tiny apartment.

As I suspected, all the buildings here were interconnected by a common roofline and I made good time for the first few hundred yards, running at right angles in the direction of the fighting . . .

heading, I hoped, directly toward the waterfront where my only chance for escape lay.

A brick wall at least ten feet tall stretched across my path, and without breaking stride I raced for it, leaping up at the last possible second, catching the top and heaving myself up.

Thirty feet below was a dark alley, and fifteen feet across was the twin to this wall. Beyond it I could see the masts of at least four or five fishing boats. I was close now.

For a moment I crouched low on the wall, catching my breath, and wondered if I could make a standing broad jump over the narrow alley. Any question of my motivation was suddenly resolved for me, however, when someone opened fire from behind, the bullets whining off the brick wall inches away from where I crouched.

In one smooth motion I stood up and jumped, hitting the top of the opposite wall somewhat off balance. I twisted to the left in a futile attempt to regain my footing, but then I was falling.

I had expected only an eight- or ten-foot drop to the roof on the other side of the wall, but as I toppled over the edge there wasn't a roof beneath me. The wall I had leaped to fronted directly on the bay, and more than forty feet below was the black, oily surface of the harbor.

Someone behind me shouted something. I caught a brief impression of the tangled wreckage of several boats and then I hit the water like an express train, plunging deep beneath the small wavelets.

A long few seconds later, I broke the surface, and for several moments I treaded water as I tried to regain my breath.

The sounds of the fighting seemed much farther away now, but a few hundred yards up the bay fires from within the city danced and wavered on the water.

After a while, I swam slowly toward the burned-out hulk of a fishing boat and then around its bow, where I grabbed the greasy anchor chain so that I could rest and figure out just what I was going to do.

The water here was warm and tasted faintly of diesel oil. As I hung there by the chain, I wondered how long it would take the soldiers who had chased me to come around here to the docks. I would be a sitting duck if they came with lights and automatic weapons.

The brick wall I had fallen from ended at the water's edge less than twenty feet away, but fifty feet farther south was a large corrugated metal boathouse, a two-foot gap beneath its tall door.

I let go of the chain and struck out toward the building, swimming in an easy breaststroke, careful to make as little noise as possible and to conserve my strength. I had a feeling I was going to need it.

Somehow I had to make it out to the sub. I only hoped that the Beersheba Nuclear Depot documents I had taken off the body of the KGB agent had not been ruined by seawater. If I could get them back to Hawk, at least partially intact, I was sure they would prove to be of Russian manufacture.

It had been a Russian setup all along. I was certain of it. But still I could not figure out why. If the KGB had wanted nuclear materials to get to the States for some reason, why hadn't they given their people their own material? It would have been a lot less risky than stealing it from the Israelis.

On top of all that was the fact that the poor slobs back in Kuwait who had handled the beta canister, evidently had no idea how dangerous the material was. Otherwise they would never have opened it.

None of this made any sense. But none of the answers would come unless I could get out of here.

At the boathouse, I ducked under the doorway, and just inside I held onto the lower edge of the big door waiting for my eyes to adjust to the deeper darkness.

Almost immediately I spotted the boat tied up at the far end of the building, its bow pointed my way. It was large, at least twenty-five feet long, and looked very slick, its black fiberglass hull and stainless steel upperworks gleaming softly in the very dim light.

I don't know what I really had expected to find. I would have been satisfied with a rubber raft or even an old rowboat; but as I swam around the bow of this vessel I knew that there would be nothing on the water, except perhaps a hydrofoil, that could catch me if I could get this one started.

Halfway back to the stern, the words SCARAB S-TYPE, were set off by a wide racing strip a couple of feet above the waterline. I had heard of this boat. It was one of the biggest and hottest production racing machines in the world, if my memory was correct. I vaguely remembered seeing one of these boats off Martha's Vineyard a year or so ago.

At the stern, I climbed up on the swim platform that stretched over twin exhaust ports that looked nearly large enough to crawl into, and then scrambled over the aft rail.

Forward, the cockpit was equipped with two deeply padded bucket seats, one of them behind a control panel that looked like it belonged on the flight deck of a jet fighter.

Between the seats was the teak hatch that led presumably to the main cabin below. And forward, through the low, racy looking windscreen, the bow deck looked like a football field-size artillery shell pointed directly at the boathouse door.

Incredibly, the ignition key was dangling from the panel. When I flipped it over to the first position, the instrument panel came alive, the fuel gauges registering full tanks.

Alarms started jangling along my nerves. No one would leave a boat like this, fully fueled, the key in the ignition, not unless they were nearby and were planning on a quick escape from the fighting.

I spun around and looked back at the dock behind me. Several boxes and a half a dozen suitcases were piled in a heap, ready to be loaded aboard. From the looks of the pile the things had been dumped there in a big hurry.

Someone *was* getting ready to leave. And very soon, unless I missed my guess.

I hurried aft, pulled out Hugo and cut the lines holding the boat to the dock, and then went back to the pilot's position.

As I was about to turn the ignition key, a door clanged open, the noise echoing throughout the building, and a half a dozen people all talking at once came in.

I had just run out of time.

I flipped the switch over, the starter motor wound up, and someone shouted something. At that moment, however, the *Scarab*'s huge engines kicked into life with an unbelievable roar, and I slammed the throttles full forward.

The speed boat seemed to leap out of the water with a tremendous surge of power, knocking me back into the bucket seat.

The doors, the single thought screamed through my mind. I just managed to duck below the level of the windscreen when the boat hit the outer door, bursting through it as if it was nothing more than papier-mache, metal and plastic flying everywhere.

Somehow I managed to regain my balance, pull myself forward and grab the wheel, hauling it way over to the left. The big boat whipped around, barely missing the wreckage of the fishing boats, inundating them with a huge spray that formed a rooster tail thirty feet high.

In the next instant I cranked the wheel to the right again, missing another tangle of wreckage, and then I was heading out to sea, the powerful boat slamming through the small waves as it continued to accelerate, leaving Beirut far behind.

Within a few minutes I had passed the harbor's outer marker, the lighthouse still functioning, the small choppy waves of the bay giving way to the bigger swells of the open sea.

I looked back, and although I could not hear the fighting over the roar of the engines, I still could see the flashes from weapons, and the fires throughout the city reflected off the water at least a mile or more into the bay.

Turning back to the controls, I found the wheel lock and cranked it into place so that the boat would hold its course unattended, straight out to sea.

I figured if I could find a radio of some sort, any

kind of a communications radio, I could send a quick signal out to the sub to expect me. The communications officer aboard the *Whiteshark* had told me that one of the sub's missions was to monitor all radio traffic in her vicinity. I was sure they would pick mine up.

The boat plunged into the trough of a wave, but this time instead of plowing through it, the engines seemed to struggle with the load and the boat shuddered as the water broke over the bow.

For a moment I studied the engine gauges, but everything seemed to be working properly as far as I could tell. Yet the boat no longer felt as lively as it had before. I was certain we had slowed down for some reason.

I slipped out of the bucket seat, and keeping a tight grip on the handholds, opened the main hatch.

There was water running below. I could hear it clearly. A lot of water.

As I started down the ladder into the dark interior of the cabin, the boat hit another trough, causing me to lose my footing, and I pitched forward into at least two feet of water.

As I scrambled to my feet, the boat hit still another wave trough, and this time seemed to dive straight down. For a long, pregnant second I was certain we were not going to recover, that we were going straight to the bottom. But then the boat struggled up out of the water, seemed to list to the right, and finally straightened out.

We were sinking. Crashing through the door of the boathouse had evidently punched a hole in the hull.

I groped around the cabin, the water already up

to my knees, until I found an overhead light switch which I flipped on. But nothing happened.

Apparently the water had already gotten to the level of the batteries and had shorted them out.

I struggled back up the ladder to the deck where I hauled back on the throttles, and the boat slowed down almost as if it had run into a brick wall. A second later the engines died, the wake caught up with us, slopping the big boat around, and we were dead in the water, slowly sinking at the bow.

Beirut was at least ten miles back, so I figured I had to be close to the sub, if only I could attract their attention somehow. I was sure they had picked me up on sonar, and if they detected the boat was sinking, they might surface long enough to investigate.

On the aft deck of the *Scarab* I found the life jackets and a small inflatable dinghy in one of the seat lockers.

The boat was sinking faster now, and by the time I had the dinghy inflated the bow was already underwater, the deck sloping sharply forward.

I tossed the small rubber raft overboard, threw a life jacket after it and jumped in myself.

By the time I had rowed less than fifty feet away, the huge speed boat had tipped straight down, its twin screws gleaming in the night, and it quietly slipped beneath the surface.

For the first minute or so a terrible sense of loneliness came over me, almost as if a huge weight was pressing down on my shoulders. But then a searchlight stabbed my way from the southwest, and I could suddenly hear the sound of a powerful engine coming toward me. For a confused moment I wondered if the *Whiteshark* carried some kind of an auxiliary launch, but then I heard a second powerful engine coming my way from a more southerly direction.

If they were Lebanese gunboats, I was a dead man.

Quickly I pulled on the life jacket and then slipped into the water. Swimming as fast as I could, I headed away from the dinghy until I had swum at least a hundred yards. Then I stopped, turned around and treaded water as the first of the two gunboats came to the raft, catching it in her spotlights.

At first I could not make out who it was, but then I caught a glimpse of the Israeli flag flying from the stern of the gunboat and I started swimming back toward the raft.

The gunboat's spotlight was centered on the rubber raft, and as I got closer I could hear someone shouting over the rumbling noise of the powerful engine.

The spotlight turned my way a second later, passed me, and then came back, the glare impossible to look at.

I stopped swimming as the boat eased my way, and then a ladder was lowered over the side and two men in Israeli Navy uniforms were helping me out of the water.

Too late I remembered the Beersheba Nuclear Depot passes in my coverall pocket.

SIX

It was nearly ten o'clock A.M. by the time the gunboat that had fished me out of the water pulled into its slip just north of Tel Aviv on the Hayarkon River.

The boat commander, a young man whose name I never did catch, had been polite but very insistent about searching me. When the Beersheba documents had been found along with my weapons, Hugo, Pierre and Wilhelmina, I was given dry dungarees, a sweatshirt and deck shoes. Then I was handcuffed.

No one had questioned me aboard, and those of the crew I had contact with treated me with a wary respect, almost as if I was some kind of a wild, very dangerous animal—interesting to look at, but from a safe distance.

A black Chevy sedan was waiting on the dock when I was led topside and directed down the ramp. Two men in civilian clothes got out of the car and the boat commander saluted them as we approached.

He handed the taller of them a duffel bag and a plain manila envelope. "The passes were pretty messed up by seawater, but they're still legible," he said.

"I understand he had quite an arsenal," the taller one said. The other civilian was staring at me.

"Nine millimeter Luger, no serial number, some kind of a dagger strapped to his forearm and something else that was strapped to his crotch."

The civilian who had been staring at me, looked at the boat commander in open amazement. "Strapped to his crotch?"

"I'd be careful with it, if I were you," I said softly. It was a powerful gas bomb that AXE's technicians had designed for me several years ago.

All three of them looked at me, but no one said a word for several long seconds. Behind me the gunboat's crew had lined up along the rail and were staring down at us.

"You did a fine job, Carl," the taller civilian said. "Are you and Carol coming over for dinner tonight?"

"We'll be there about eight," the boat commander said.

"See you then," the civilian said, and then he took me by my right elbow and led me over to the car where I climbed in the back seat. They locked the door behind me. Both of them climbed in the front seat and we took off into Tel Aviv.

"Do you have a name?" the one driving asked me after we had cleared the Naval yard. He was looking at me in the rearview mirror.

"Nick Carter," I said absently. I hoped the *Whiteshark* had witnessed what happened. If they had, they'd be contacting the blind number at State that would be routed to Hawk.

"Just who do you work for, Mr. Carter?" the driver asked.

"The U.S. Atomic Energy Commission," I said. "I don't suppose we could swing by the U.S. Embassy for a chat?"

The man in the passenger seat turned around and smiled at me. The gesture totally devoid of humor. "We'd like to have a little chat with you first, Mr. Carter, or whoever you really are," he said sarcastically. "We're all just dying to find out what you were doing in Beirut, and how you happened to come by Israeli military documents."

"No more curious than we are about your nuclear depot at Beersheba," I snapped.

The man struck out at me, but I had anticipated his move and managed to fall back far enough so that his backhand did not connect.

"How about taking off the cuffs?" I said.

"We don't take kindly to spies in our country," he said between clenched teeth.

"I wasn't in your country."

"You had our military documents, and before we're done your smart mouth will be gone, and we'll have the answers we want."

"Rubber truncheons, electric probes under my fingernails and all that sort of thing?"

"Just a shot of happy juice, and you'll tell us what we want to know."

It was the one thing I was afraid of and it must have shown on my face, because the man in the passenger seat grinned. If they put me under some kind of truth serum, they'd learn who I really was. They'd find out about AXE and its organizational chart, about Hawk, about everything. I could not allow that to happen.

"We're going to Bilu Street," I said softly. "Number twenty-four." It was the secret headquarters of the Mossad, Israel's intelligence service.

A startled expression crossed the man's features, and the driver turned around to look at me, almost running the car off the road before he recovered.

"What the hell—" the man in the passenger seat started to sputter but I cut him off.

"I'll have to speak with Dov Hacherut," I said, naming the Mossad's new chief. There were very few people in the world who knew the identity of the top Mossad administrator.

The effect that my knowledge had on them wiped the smile off the man's face. He turned around in his seat, and we drove the rest of the way into the city in silence, pulling into a small parking lot behind a three-story building on Bilu Street.

I was taken through a back door where my guards signed in with the security clerk, and then we went up to the third floor where I was left alone in a soundproof interrogation room with no windows, and only a small metal table and three chairs.

Five minutes later one of the men who had picked me up at the Navy yard came into the room, asked me my clothing sizes and then left again.

A couple of minutes after that he was back, and without a word, he took off the handcuffs that had been holding my hands tightly behind my back, dropped a pack of filter-tipped Time cigarettes and a book of matches on the table, and left again.

I sat back in the chair, rubbed my wrists to get the circulation going again and then lit myself a cigarette, the first since before I had gone ashore at Beirut more than eight hours ago.

Elsewhere in the building at this moment there

would be a series of hastily called conferences. A message would be sent to the State Department in Washington, and I was pretty certain that even the prime minister here would be informed about me.

What was an American doing in Beirut? What was he doing with Beersheba Nuclear Depot passes? How in hell did he know the name of our chief and the location if our offices?

What was going on?

Even more dust would fly when they discovered that the military passes were Russian forgeries. I was sure they had been in a panicked flap about the missing beta canister. But now to add to their confusion they had a knowledgeable American on their hands with Russian-made documents.

Which left the *Akai Maru.* Fortunately, the decision to either withhold that information from the Israelis or tell them, would be made at diplomatic levels. But unless I could get out of here and soon, other more drastic measures would have to be taken, with the risk that the strontium 90 would be dumped overboard in the ocean.

Dov Hacherut was a tall, husky man of at least sixty. His hair was graying and mussed, his tie was loose, and his suit looked as if he had slept in it for the last week.

When he came in alone, he was carrying a small canvas traveling bag, which he laid on the table. He did not look happy.

"Good morning," I said, stubbing out my cigarette and getting to my feet.

He just glared at me and then opened the travel bag. Inside was a suit, shirt, tie, shoes and socks as well as several documents.

"Fresh clothing," he said, his voice guttural. "A

fresh diplomatic passport, your wallet and identification, airline tickets, one way to Athens, Greece.
Your plane leaves in an hour and a half. As soon as
you're dressed you'll be taken out to the airport."

"My weapons?" I asked.

"Confiscated."

"The Beersheba passes?"

Something flashed in the man's eyes. "Israeli
property," he snapped. He leaned forward, shoved
the travel bag aside, and placed both his hands on
the table, knuckles down. "You have been declared
persona non grata, Mr. Carter. I suggest you give us
absolutely no trouble over the next couple of
hours. And I strongly suggest you never return to
this country."

"We're allies," I said.

"Have I made myself clear?" Hacherut asked.

I nodded.

Commander Bob Jordan was waiting for me
when I cleared customs at Athens' Hellenikon Airport around three in the afternoon, local time. He
didn't seem as jolly as he had on our first meeting,
for which small favor I was grateful. I was dead
tired and in no mood for his levity.

Hawk had instructed me to keep this mission
low key, but just the opposite had happened in
Kuwait. He had also warned me that we could not
afford to step on any toes, but the Israelis had been
placed in the embarrassing position of knowing
that we knew about their nuclear depot.

No doubt Hacherut was under the gun from
above, which explained his foul mood. The
diplomatic wires between Tel Aviv and Washing-

ton would be alive with activity, in what the boys at State would be terming a "non-media incident." None of this would ever get in the newspapers.

"I have a car and driver out front for you, sir," Jordan said. I followed him through the busy terminal and outside to where the plain gray Navy sedan was parked.

"Take me to the embassy please," I said when we climbed in the back seat. I was going to have to get a message off to Hawk to see if he still wanted me aboard the *Akai Maru*, and if so, to set the Navy wheels in motion.

"Belay that order," Jordan said to the driver. "We're going to one-oh-one." He seemed uncomfortable. "Sorry, sir," he said turning to me. "I was ordered to meet you here and get you over to the hangar."

"By whom?" I asked.

"I don't know, sir," he said. "The orders came from Washington."

"How far out is the *Whiteshark* this time?" I asked.

Jordan seemed startled. "She's in about the same position as the first time you went out to her," he said. "She's clear of any Russian vessels this time," he quickly added.

The man was really trying, and I suppose I had been hard on him the last time, so I smiled. "Thanks for the help, commander."

"Yes, sir," he replied. We rode the rest of the way across the airport in silence pulling into the open hangar where the same Sikorsky helicopter as before was waiting for me.

When we got out of the car I shook Jordan's hand. "Thanks again for the help, commander.

And if I was a little rough on you the first time, I'm sorry. I was under a lot of pressure."

"I understand, sir," the man said, obviously relieved that I was not going to give him any trouble. "Good luck."

I turned, went across to the helicopter and climbed aboard. David Hawk was seated in one of the passenger seats, a glum look on his face.

"Strap in, the *Whiteshark* is holding position for us," he said.

As I climbed into the seat next to his and fastened my seat belt, a ground crewman closed the helicopter door, and we were rolling toward the takeoff area outside.

Within a couple of minutes the main engine came to life, the rotors began to spin and we were lifting off, any talk difficult because of the noise.

Hawk leaned my way nevertheless. "How do you feel?" he shouted.

"Tired," I shouted back. "And surprised that you're here, sir."

He didn't smile. "All hell is breaking loose. We're going to have to move very fast now."

"The *Akai Maru*?" I shouted, and he nodded.

"She'll be clearing Gibraltar in a few hours. We'll rendezvous around midnight tomorrow. Should give you plenty of time to rest."

"Yes, sir," I said.

For several long seconds Hawk stared at me, a strange expression on his face. He leaned a little closer. "Bridley and McQueen are dead," he shouted.

"What?" I asked, my stomach flopping over.

Hawk nodded. "Bridley's son died before they could bring him home. The father came unglued, took a gun and shot McQueen to death, then blew his own brains out."

I sat way back in my seat, a sharp picture in my mind of Bridley seated behind his desk, the bottle of Chivas Regal in front of him as he talked about his son.

How many people had died so far in this thing? There was the man at the embassy gate, and the Marine guard who had gotten too close to him. There was the woman and the two men in the Kuwait City apartment, as well as Bridley's son and the other Marine who had gone up there at McQueen's order. If young Bridley had died of radiation poisoning, it was a sure bet the other Marine would die as well.

There was the Muslim guard on the roof in Beirut as well as the two people in the apartment and the two KGB agents.

And now Bridley himself and McQueen.

How many more would there be, I asked myself. And for what purpose?

We went the rest of the way out to the submarine in silence, until about forty-five minutes later when the co-pilot came back to us.

"The sub will be surfacing in just a few moments, sir," he said to Hawk. "Are you sure you want to try this?"

Hawk had unbuckled his seatbelt, and he got to his feet. "Sure thing, son," he said. "I'll go first."

The young man shrugged, said "Yes, sir," and then helped Hawk strap into a harness which was hooked to a cable wound around a winch drum.

At the main hatch he put on a headset, spoke into the microphone, and a moment later shoved the door open, the interior of the helicopter instantly filling with wind and noise. He swung the winch arm out and then helped Hawk to the opening.

"Good luck, sir," he shouted, and Hawk stepped out. For a moment he dangled there, the wind buffeting his body, but then the young lieutenant released the winch motor and Hawk dropped slowly out of sight.

Within five minutes the harness was back and I strapped in. Before I stepped out, I shouted, "Thanks for the ride," to the co-pilot, and I was being lowered to the deck of the submarine about seventy-five feet below.

Hawk was already drinking a cup of coffee with Captain Farmington in the officers' wardroom when I was hustled below, and we immediately submerged.

When I entered the tiny compartment, Farmington stood up, nodded at me, then turned back to Hawk. "I'll see you on the bridge when you're finished here, sir."

"I want you to get us there as quickly as you can, Newton," Hawk said.

"Aye aye, sir," Farmington replied, and then he left us, closing the door behind him.

Hawk's face was red and his hair was windblown, but other than that he didn't look much the worse for wear.

I poured myself a cup of coffee and sat down across the table from him.

"That was quite an experience," he said.

"Yes, sir," I answered.

"Captain Farmington asked me to convey his apologies for not being able to pick you up before the Israelis got to you. But he said by the time they figured out it was probably you aboard the speedboat, the Israelis were already in your vicinity and he had to sit tight."

"I understand," I said. "But I'm afraid I created quite a stir in Tel Aviv."

"Indeed," Hawk said. He took out a cigar, unwrapped it, and when he had it lit, he sat back. "The President had to admit to Mr. Begin that we knew about their Beersheba reactor. No one was happy about it."

"Was the *Akai Maru* mentioned?"

"Fortunately not," Hawk said. "Although the President was prepared to discuss the issue if Begin brought it up. But they did mention something about some kind of Israeli military documents. That seemed to upset them even more than our knowledge of the reactor."

"They're going to be even more upset when they find out the passes are Russian forgeries."

Hawk sat forward. "What?" he said, the single word sharp, almost like a pistol shot.

Quickly I recounted for him everything that had happened to me from the moment I left the sub and entered Beirut. When I got to the part about the two KGB agents in the apartment, the color seemed to drain out of his cheeks.

"Kobelev," he said half under his breath.

"Sir?"

For a long moment Hawk did not seem to be aware of anything around him, but then he blinked and focused on me. "Nikolai Fedor Kobelev. Six months ago he was appointed head of the KGB's First Chief Directorate's Executive Action Department. Code name Puppet Master."

"Do you think he's behind this?"

"If he is, we're in bigger trouble than I thought we were." Hawk stubbed out his cigar in the ashtray and got to his feet. "I'm going to have to call the President immediately. When the Israelis discover that the Beersheba passes are forgeries, they're going to suspect that we made the strike on the depot. We're going to have to tell them about the Russians."

"What about this Kobelev, sir?" I asked.

"He's a brilliant man, but probably the most anti-Western voice within Kremlin politics. Since Vietnam, he's been the power behind the rising sentiment in the Soviet Union that they could win an all-out nuclear war with us. Fortunately there are enough moderates in control at the moment to hold him down. Six months ago when we learned that he had been named chief of the Executive Action Department, we all held our breath waiting for him to do something big. It hasn't happened. At least not until now."

"But why put nuclear material aboard an oil carrier?"

"I don't know, Nick," Hawk said. "You're going to have to find that out when you board the *Akai Maru* tomorrow night."

He went to the door, but before he left the wardroom he turned back to me, an intensely worried look in his eyes. "You're going to have to be extra careful this time, Nick. Kobelev is good. The best. If he suspects you're aboard the *Akai Maru*, he'll stop at nothing to get you. The man has never been known to do anything slipshod. He's the very best."

"I'll need new weapons and another Geiger counter," I said.

Hawk nodded. "We're rendezvousing with a re-supply ship just off Gibraltar. They're bringing your things. I want you to get some rest now, you're going to need it."

It was a few minutes after midnight and the *Whiteshark*'s bridge was bathed in the soft red glow of her battle lights. Captain Farmington was at the periscope, his arms draped over the range and focus handles.

"Two degrees starboard bow planes," he said softly, and the helmsman complied.

Hawk and I stood together behind the chart table out of everyone's way. This afternoon we had made contact with our re-supply ship, which had brought me fresh weapons from Washington, along with a new Geiger counter and a thick batch of files from AXE's archives. The things had been flown by an Air Force fighter-interceptor from Andrews Air Force Base in Washington, to an aircraft carrier in the Mediterranean, and from there by helicopter to us just after we had entered the Atlantic.

The files included material on Kobelev as well as dossiers and photos of known or suspected members of the Lebanese terrorist group, the Red Fist of November.

The dead woman in the Kuwait apartment, as well as Hermil Zahle in Beirut, had been among the organization's leadership council. For a couple of hours I studied the files in detail, fixing in my mind as many of the faces from the photos as I could.

"They're presumably working for Kobelev," Hawk told me. "If that's the case, and any of them are aboard the *Akai Maru*, their orders will be to kill anyone who interferes with them."

There was a wealth of material in Kobelev's file, but most of it was speculative detail from AXE and CIA foreign watchers. If even half of what the analysts suspected Kobelev had been behind was true, however, he was a diabolical, ruthless man who had absolutely no regard for human life. For any life.

"Range, mark," Farmington said from the periscope. "Computer?"

"Two hundred yards and closing, slowly," the computer operator called from his console.

"Sonar?" Farmington called out softly.

"She's making twenty-two-point-five knots, our relative speeds are closing."

"Give me two percent on the midships tanks," the captain said.

"Aye aye, sir," the helmsman said, and after a few seconds he added. "Mark. Sixty feet."

"Computer?"

"One hundred fifty yards and continuing to close."

"Sonar?"

"Relative speeds at match, differential only at the angle."

Farmington straightened up and turned around. "Are you ready, Mr. Carter?"

"Yes sir," I said coming around the chart table. I picked up the haversack off the deck and strapped it on my back, making sure the shoulder harnesses were tight. Then I pulled on the leather gloves. I was wearing a black Navy commando coverall set, and had again blackened my face.

"Mr. Jacobs to the bridge with the launcher, on

the double," Farmington said into the boat's intercom, and then he turned back to the periscope.

"Sonar?"

"Holding sir."

"Computer?"

"Seventy-five yards, continuing to close."

"Give it to me by fives."

"Aye aye, sir," the computer operator said. Now there was a tenseness on the bridge, and everywhere through the boat we could hear the drumming of the oil tanker's screws overhead. A slight miscalculation, a current surge, the tiniest of malfunctions could slew us into the mammoth vessel plowing through the water above us at better than twenty knots.

"Seventy yards, mark," the computer operator called out.

"Give me two degrees rudder offset to counteract the surge currents on the mark," Farmington said.

"Aye aye, sir," the helmsman replied.

"Sixty-five yards, mark."

"Sonar?"

"Our speeds are matched, sir."

"Sixty yards mark."

"Rudder offset," Farmington said.

"Fifty-five yards, mark," the computer operator called out.

"Mark the rudder," Farmington said.

"Rudder at two degrees, sir."

"Fifty yards mark," the computer operator said. "Fifty yards. Fifty yards, holding."

Farmington again straightened up from the periscope. "Bring us to fifty feet," he said. "Computer, keep a close watch on our separation."

"Aye aye, sir," both men said almost simultaneously, and Farmington came across to me.

"There's an eight-foot swell running up there, under a wind of ten to fifteen knots, Mr. Carter. Is this a go?"

"Yes, sir," I said.

Arnold Jacobs the burly chief from maintenance came onto the bridge carrying the grappling hook launcher and climbing gear. I had talked with him earlier about what had to be done and I was convinced he knew what he was doing.

"Set to go, Mr. Carter?" he said smiling at me.

"Any time you're ready, chief," I said.

"Listen up," Farmington said to his men on the bridge. "As soon as we surface and the hatch comes open I'll want absolute attention down here. I'll be controlling the boat from topside. As soon as Mr. Carter is away we'll be getting out of here. We're going to be damned close to the tanker, so everyone look alive." He looked at his men. "Questions?"

There were none.

"Good luck," Hawk said to me.

"Bring us to forty feet," Farmington said.

"Aye aye, sir," the helmsman said, and everyone watched the digital readout over the man's position as the numbers flickered down to forty and then stopped.

"Green light on the hatch, sir," the deck officer said.

"Let's get it over with then," Farmington said, and he scrambled up the ladder into the conning tower. A few seconds later we could hear the sounds of the sea, of the huge tanker nearby, plowing through it, and could smell the fresh outside air.

Jacobs was next up the ladder and then I was following him.

The *Akai Maru*, fifty yards away rose up like a sheer, impregnable wall, the water streaming off its bow a few yards ahead of us, boiling with a soft white luminescence.

Farmington plugged in a headset and spoke briefly into the microphone, but I could not hear what he was saying because of the noise from the tanker.

Within a couple of minutes we had edged a little closer to the huge vessel and our position once again seemed to stabilize. Farmington looked at me. "Thirty yards is the best we can do under these conditions. Is it still a go, Mr. Carter?"

I nodded.

Farmington looked at me for a long moment, then he too nodded. "Good luck," he said. He turned to Jacobs. "Go."

The chief braced himself, raised the launcher to his shoulder and fired, the blast lost to the noise of the tanker's motion through the sea.

The wire whined out of the spool, slowed down and then stopped, and Jacobs was reeling it in until it was snug. Next he clamped the climbing device onto the wire and held the foot and hand grips out to me.

"I think you're outa' your friggin' mind, Mr. Carter, if you don't mind me saying so. But good luck anyway."

"Thanks, chief," I said, then I made sure my pack was tight, the slack had been taken up on the wire, and the grips levered as far up the wire as I could reach, climbed up on the wide rail, the chief steadying me, raised the grips one more time, took a deep breath, and jumped.

SEVEN

The one thing we had not anticipated was the combined effect of the tanker's bow wave and the eight-foot swells that were running.

As I swung in a low arc toward the hull of the *Akai Maru* I had less than two seconds to realize that I was going to be hit by the top of a twelve-foot wave moving at around twenty-five knots, and I just managed to tighten my hold on the grips when it came.

I was slammed violently to the left, the moving water dragging and tearing at my body, my arms nearly pulling out of their sockets.

At the instant I was certain I would be swept away, the wave dropped below me, I was spun around and I hit the side of the ship with my back, the haversack absorbing some of the blow.

The ship continued to rise up out of the water as I quickly began sliding the grips upward, shifting my weight from one to the other, climbing as fast as I could as the ship began its plunge downward.

Another wave would definitely pull me off the wire, and for a seeming eternity it looked as if I could not win this race. Then the wave passed a couple of feet beneath me and the ship climbed up again on the next crest.

For a long time I remained where I was, swaying in fifty-foot arcs with the motion of the ship, the waves alternately coming within a couple of feet from me and then dropping away twenty or thirty feet below.

Behind me the submarine had already submerged and I supposed at this moment Farmington was watching me through the periscope, although I could not make out anything from where I hung by the thin wire.

I looked up, but the rail of the ship seemed to be a hundred miles overhead, and I could see no indication of the bow light. She must have been running dark, which many vessels did at sea, contrary to international law.

After a while I began climbing again, slowly this time, making sure my grip was tight and the clamps were fully engaged before I shifted my weight each time to the upper unit.

As I came higher up the side of the vessel the wind began to swirl around me, forcing me into a spin and swinging me into increasingly shorter and faster arcs.

My arms and legs now were so tired that each move I made had to be done with great deliberation and even then I slipped more than once, nearly losing my grip and plunging downward to certain death, either by drowning, or to be mangled in the gigantic propellers.

Time seemed to have no meaning for me then. Whenever I looked up to check my progress, the bow rail seemed to be getting no closer; always it seemed to be miles overhead.

I'd rest for a couple of minutes then and continue climbing, the backpack pulling me down, my hands and the insteps of my feet on fire from the narrow stirrups of the grips.

What seemed an eternity later, about the time I was sure I could not continue, the upper grip became stuck and I looked up. The wire was gone and the handle of the grip was wedged against a thick metal bar. For several seconds I stared stupidly at the handle, wondering where the hell the wire was, if it had broken somewhere above, and why I wasn't falling. But then I looked forward and realized I was seeing the bow deck of the *Akai Maru*. I had made it. Somehow I had gotten to the top.

Mindless of the danger that I could be spotted from the bridge, I clambered clumsily over the rail and fell into a heap on the deck, my breath coming in ragged gasps, my arms and legs shaking with fatigue.

The wind felt good across my body now, although the air smelled strongly of crude oil. Slowly my heart began to stop its rapid pounding. Once again I had beat the odds. Once again I had made it. But something else seemed to intrude on my numbed brain, something Hawk had warned me about during my briefing this afternoon when we had studied the architects' drawings of the ship.

"Once you're over the rail, Nick, you're going to have to get rid of the grappling hook and line, and then get below before someone spots you."

Before I was spotted. Hawk's words seemed to ring in my ears as if he was beside me, and I opened my eyes with a start.

I was lying on my back and nearly a thousand feet aft. The ship's superstructure, gleaming white in the night, rose eight stories up from the deck. At the highest level the wide glass windows were lit with a soft red glow. The bridge. Had someone spotted me already?

My mind was starting to come back into focus now and I rolled over to the rail. I very carefully unhooked the grapple from where it had caught on the top bar of the rail and let it go over the side.

Keeping low, I crawled slowly from the edge, finding the bow hatch almost immediately. This would be the critical point for me now that I was aboard. If I could get the hatch open, get below and close it again without being spotted by anyone on the bridge, or by a crewman on deck, I would be relatively safe.

For a long moment I studied the line of windows in the superstructure, then carefully undogged the hatch, lifted it up just far enough for me to slip inside, and then closed and re-dogged it from below.

I was in absolute darkness here, but from the ship's diagrams I had studied I knew that I was now standing on a narrow platform from which a ladder descended sixty feet to a wide corridorlike catwalk that was called L-Deck Forward.

From the lower catwalk, entry could be gained to a number of maintenance positions where the bow condition detectors were located, as well as the forecastle compartment itself which contained the vessel's odds and ends: spare oil line pumps and the equipment to replace them, spare hull and hold plates along with the welding gear to make temporary repairs, and other such things.

Unless the ship ran into some kind of serious trouble, however, no one would ever come down to the dark, dank compartment just above the bulbous bow of the ship.

Across the L-Deck Forward catwalk from the forecastle compartment, were the maintenance and access tunnels for the tanker's holds themselves. Through the maze of passageways I would have nearly free access to almost any part of the ship day or night.

I stood for a few moments listening to the sounds of the huge ship, then I took a small penlight from one of the zippered pockets in my coveralls and shined it down. The light only illuminated the first couple of rungs of the ladder, but it was enough for me to start down. I went the rest of the way by feel.

I swung into an easy rhythm climbing down the ladder, taking it one rung at a time. I forced myself, however, to descend slowly. The motion of the ship as she plowed through the sea was strong here at the bow, and after coming this far, I did not want to end up splattered over some catwalk deep within the bowels of an oil tanker.

None of us knew quite what to expect aboard this ship, but I had been supplied with another of the high-frequency signalling units, and the *Whiteshark* would be standing by a few miles off in case I ran into any trouble, or in case I had to get off the ship in a hurry.

The major problem, of course, was going to be the strontium 90 itself. It had been taken out of its canister and unless it had been repacked in another lead-lined container, it would be too hot for me to approach let alone steal and then get it to the *Whiteshark*.

The first step would be for me to set up my operational headquarters in the forecastle compartment and then begin an inch by inch search of the entire vessel. If and when I found the strontium 90, I would have to figure out how I was going to get it to the *Whiteshark*.

I had been climbing down for nearly five minutes when my left foot touched a wide, flat surface instead of a ladder rung. Holding tightly with one hand, I took the penlight out with the other and shined it around. I had made it to L-Deck Forward.

Stepping away from the ladder I loosened the straps of the pack and swung it off my back. From within I took out a large flashlight and switched it on, pocketing the tiny penlight.

The L-Deck catwalk ran the width of the ship. Above, the ladder was attached to the wall of the access tunnel that was ten feet in diameter. Below, through the open mesh floor, I could see a maze of pipelines, valves and pumps. To the left was a wall of welded steel plates, beyond which was five million gallons of crude oil. To the right, following the sweeping curve of the bow, were a series of small oval hatches, leading, I suspected, to the various maintenance compartments.

Carrying the heavy backpack in one hand and the powerful flashlight in the other, I turned to the right, ducked under a low bulkhead and went into a large open area that was filled with pipelines for the bow intake fittings. On the opposite side from where I stood was a large hatch that led into the forecastle compartment itself.

I crossed the pipeline area, undogged the hatch and stepped into the compartment, pausing on the threshold to play my light over the various crates, piles of hold plates and what appeared to be a length of huge anchor chain. Then I went all the way in and closed the hatch behind me. The room was fairly large, at least twenty feet on a side, with a low ceiling. It was cold, damp and smelled strongly of crude oil—a smell, I unhappily realized that I was going to have to live with for as long as I was aboard.

Farther into the compartment I stepped around a pile of heavy wooden crates, intending to stow my gear out of sight of the hatchway in case a crewman should happen to look inside for some reason, but I was stopped in my tracks.

Just behind the crates was a sleeping bag laid out on the deck. Alongside it was a battery driven lantern, a backpack and a cardboard box that contained C rations.

Someone else was hiding aboard the *Akai Maru*. But who? And why?

I laid my pack alongside the sleeping bag and went through the things that had already been set up. There was no identification, nor was there any equipment that indicated the nationality of the person using this place. The C rations were just that, American military field rations. But practically anyone in the world who wanted to buy C rations could do so at any surplus store. The clothing was all dark, and there were spare batteries of French manufacture and two boxes of .380 caliber Italian ammunition.

The one thing that struck me about the clothing, however, was the size. It was all meant for a very small person. Japanese was my first thought. But this was a legitimate Japanese ship. Why would one of their own people be hiding here?

Another thing that struck me as odd, were the batteries. There were several different sizes. Some of them quite small but powerful. Nowhere, however, could I find any electronic equipment that might require such batteries. My first thought was a communications radio; my second thought was a Geiger counter.

Taking my pack, I stepped back around the crates and took up position in a corner of the compartment to the left of the hatch. I hunched down, took out my Luger, and after a moment, flipped my flashlight off.

For several seconds red and white spots danced in front of my eyes, but they finally faded, and although I could not see a thing in the absolute darkness, I had the direction of the hatch firmly fixed in my mind. And I settled down to wait.

Sometime later I looked at the luminous dials of my watch: it was 3:30. The dawn would be coming soon, which meant that I would have to remain here through the day. I could not go poking around the ship until I found out who else was aboard, and I was assuming that whoever it was would be coming back to this compartment before the morning crew started its duties.

I was about to raise my hand to look at my watch for the second time, when there was a faint noise at the hatch and I stiffened, bringing my Luger up and snapping the safety off.

The hatch swung open and the beam of a flashlight stabbed the darkness as someone came into the compartment, closed the hatch and re-dogged it.

I could just barely make out the figure of someone in dark clothing and a dark cap, and then the person turned and went around the crates, bending down out of sight for a moment.

A brighter light came on illuminating half the compartment, and the person stood up and pulled off the stocking cap. Long sandy-blonde hair cascaded down her shoulders as she shook her head.

It was a woman. For a long, stunned moment I stared directly into her face. She could not see me because I was still hidden in the deep shadows across the room, but I could see her perfectly.

She threw the cap down, unzippered the front of her coveralls and stepped out of them before I could do a thing. Underneath she wore only a bra and panties, and although I felt like a peeping Tom, I had to admit she had a fine body; trim and lithe, a slight bronze cast to her skin.

"Lovely," I said softly as I stood up.

She snapped my way, and a split second later dropped behind the crates and the compartment was plunged into total darkness.

I leaped to the left, hitting the deck and rolling twice as she fired what sounded like a silenced pistol, the shot ricocheting several times around the compartment.

"You'll kill us both," I shouted, as I rolled again to the left. I did not want her to pinpoint the direction of my voice.

She fired another shot, this one careening with a high-pitched whine, just to my right.

For a long while then the compartment was silent, with only the thrumming of the engines coming from a long ways off. Carefully, so as to make absolutely no noise, I reached into my coverall pocket and withdrew the penlight. The line of crates was less than ten feet straight out in front of me, and unless she had moved, which I didn't think she had, she would still be there.

Slowly, I gathered my feet up under me and raised myself in a half crouch. Next I flipped the Luger's safety back on and stuffed the gun in my shoulder holster.

Taking a deep breath I flipped the penlight on and threw it to the left at the same instant I leaped forward.

I caught just a vague glimpse of the woman standing behind the crates as the tiny beam from the penlight flipped crazily end over end, as she fired in its direction. In the next instant I was over the crates crashing into her, knocking her back onto her sleeping bag and backpack in a tangle of bare arms and legs.

She was strong and very quick, but no match for my superior weight, and within a couple of frantic moments I had her pinned to the deck, my left hand at her throat, and the fingers of my right hand bending the wrist of her gun hand forward. At the same time I tried to keep out of the way of her fingernails of her free hand as she tried to scratch my eyes out.

"I'll break your wrist unless you calm down," I snapped harshly.

She renewed her struggles and I applied more pressure to her wrist. At any moment it would have to snap, something I did not want to happen, but she was leaving me no choice. I applied even more pressure and she finally cried out, and slumped back.

"All right," she said. Her voice was soft, her English tinged with a slight Hebrew accent. Israeli?

She dropped the gun to the deck, but I continued to hold pressure on her wrist. "Who are you?" I asked.

"You're hurting me," she said.

I laughed. "You tried to kill me and damned near succeeded. Who are you? Mossad?"

She stiffened. I was certain she was going to try again to dislodge me, so I clamped down harder on her wrist, and she cried out.

"I'm a friend, damnit," I hissed. "I spoke with Hacherut less than forty-eight hours ago. We're here for the same thing. It has to be obvious by now that I'm not one of the crew."

The fight seemed to go out of her then and she whimpered. "You're hurting me," she said softly.

I eased the pressure on her wrist and started to swing my left leg off her, when she heaved up shoving me to one side, sending me crashing into the crates.

As I tried to regain my balance something very hard slammed into the side of my head causing me to see stars, and I swung blindly in the dark with my right fist, catching her squarely on the jaw, and she went down.

For a long time I sat there, my back up against the crates trying to regain my balance, my head spinning and my stomach churning.

Finally I crawled forward, found the battery-driven lantern and switched it on.

The young woman lay flat on her back, her bra torn half off her lovely breasts and a large angry welt forming on her jaw.

I crawled over to her, afraid for a moment that I had killed her, but her breathing was regular and her eyes were starting to flutter.

Setting the light down I pulled her around, laid her in her sleeping bag, flipped the cover over her and zippered it up. Trussed in like that she wouldn't be able to make any fast moves once she came around. And besides, it was cold down here.

She finally opened her eyes and seemed disoriented for a few seconds. When she focused on me she tried to struggle out of her bag.

"I don't normally hit women, but if you don't settle down I'll give you the thrashing of your life."

She glared at me, but then slumped back in the sleeping bag. A moment later her hand came up and she rubbed her jaw.

"You didn't leave me much choice," I said. I was feeling guilty about hitting her.

"Who are you? Why are you aboard this ship?" she asked harshly.

"You've got it backward, sweetheart," I said. "I'm asking the questions. Who are you?"

"Sharon Neumann."

"I'm Nick Carter, pleased to meet you," I said. "And now there's the matter of who you work for, how you got aboard this ship and what you're doing here."

Her nostrils flared, but she said nothing.

She had been carrying a small haversack when she had come through the hatch. I bent down and picked it up. She struggled wildly with the sleeping bag and was halfway out of it before I had my Luger out and pointed at her. She slumped back.

I laid her pack on one of the crates and opened it with one hand, keeping the Luger pointed in her general direction with the other. I had absolutely no intention of shooting her unless I was forced into it.

From within the pack I pulled out a small radio, somewhat similar in design to the one I was carrying, and next to it in a leather case was a Geiger counter. She too was here for the strontium 90.

I replaced the things in her pack and turned my full attention back to her. "Which means you're either working for the Israeli secret service or for the Red Fist of November. Which is it?"

Something sparked deep within her eyes. "I am an Israeli."

"Mossad?"

She nodded uncertainly.

"Who's your boss?"

"Hacherut," she said.

I had to laugh. "I already mentioned the name. You're going to have to do better than that," I told her. "If it makes it any easier for you, I work for the U.S. Atomic Energy Commission. I know your boss's name and where his office is located. I spoke with him less than forty-eight hours ago."

"Dov Hacherut," she said after a moment. "Bilu Street, Tel Aviv."

I relaxed and stuffed the Luger back in its holster, then lit a cigarette and offered it to her.

She hesitated a moment, but then accepted it. When I had one lit for myself, I again sat back on one of the crates.

"We're both here for the strontium 90 that the Red Fist of November lifted from your Beersheba Depot," I said.

"It's Israeli property."

"Heading for the United States."

"How did you find out about it?" she asked.

I told her about the incident at the Kuwait embassy, but did not go into any detail about what had happened in Beirut.

"But how did you get aboard?" she asked looking sharply at me.

"Over the rail from the sea."

She shook her head and started to say something, but then bit it off. A moment later she said, "Extraordinary."

"It wasn't much," I said.

She waved my comment aside. "I don't mean that, I mean the fact I believe you."

I had to laugh at that. "Now it's your turn again. How'd you trace the strontium 90 to this ship, and how did you get aboard?"

"I don't know for sure how the canister was traced here, if it ever was," she said. "But within a few hours after the Beersheba strike, the order went out that everyone in the field was to closely watch the activities of the Red Fist of November. We had people in Beirut, but they dropped out of sight three days ago."

"You were working in Kuwait?" I asked.

She nodded. "I've been there for the past eighteen months."

"You boarded this ship in Kuwait then, before she sailed?"

Again the young woman nodded.

"But why?"

"Two Red Fist members signed on as crew three weeks ago. I'd been watching them on and off for the entire time. When the word came out about the organization's connection with the theft of a beta canister, I reported in, was sent a radio and Geiger counter and ordered aboard."

"To find the strontium 90, and then what?"

She seemed a little uncomfortable with this last

question, so I answered it for her. "There's an Israeli Navy vessel following us?"

"No," she said. "Transport planes and airliners. There's a schedule of flyovers. If I find anything I'm to radio up."

I don't know why, but I did not believe this last part. But I could not figure out why she would lie about something like that when she had apparently told me the truth about everything else.

"Have you found it yet?" I asked.

"No," she admitted after a very long hesitation. "I think my Geiger counter is malfunctioning."

"What makes you suspect that?"

"I'm reading low level radiation almost everywhere aboard the ship. Nothing dangerous, just a continuous low level reading. The canister should show up as a hot spot somewhere."

My stomach flopped over. The empty beta canister had been in the apartment in Kuwait City. I suddenly knew where the strontium 90 itself had been put. Still, it made no sense.

"Get dressed," I snapped. I turned and went back to where I had left my backpack and was about to open it to get my Geiger counter when I heard a noise directly overhead. It had sounded like someone had dropped something.

I held my breath for a long second, looking up at the ceiling. A moment later there were footsteps slowly crossing the deck above.

Sharon had heard them as well, and when I went back to her, she had her gun in hand and was looking up at the ceiling.

"Stay here," I said softly, "I'll go out and see." I turned and went back to the hatch as she doused the light.

I remained by the closed hatch for a full minute until my eyes were fully adjusted to the absolute darkness, and then softly undogged the latch and eased the hatch open.

There were dim reflections of a light out in the L-Deck catwalk area, and as I crossed the pipeline room the light seemed to waver and then turned away toward the left.

Someone was out there, one deck above, with a flashlight. But why down here? Unless they had spotted me coming aboard.

I edged around the corner and looked down the catwalk as the light flashed in the access tunnel. I did not want to interfere with any of the regular crew, only with the two Red Fist members who had signed on three weeks ago. But if whoever was coming down the tunnel headed for the forecastle compartment, I'd have to stop them. What would happen after that would be anyone's guess.

Careful not to make any noise, I slipped out onto the L-Deck catwalk and started to the right. I was intending to hide behind some of the pipelines that led into the main holds, when something hard slammed into the side of my head at the same spot where Sharon's gun had struck me, and a million tiny lights burst in my eyes before everything went dim.

EIGHT

In stages I became aware that I was lying on my back on something firm and that there was a very bright light directly overhead. Then something sharp jabbed at the wound in my head and I jerked away.

Someone very close said something in Japanese which I didn't quite catch, and then a pair of powerful hands, smelling faintly of cinnamon, were holding my head steadily to one side.

I opened my eyes as once more something sharp jabbed at the wound on my head and I jerked.

"If you don't hold still I'll not be able to make this last stitch," a man's voice that held a strong Japanese accent said from above me.

"All right," I said, forcing myself to relax.

"You do speak English," the doctor said, and the jabbing pain came again. A few moments later the doctor said, "Let him go," in Japanese.

I had picked up the language after several assignments in Japan some years ago. I still had a girlfriend who ran AXE's Tokyo operation, and although my command of the idiom wasn't perfect, I could follow most conversations.

The man holding my head released his grip and

stepped back. He was short but was built like a bull. He was dressed all in white. I turned and looked up at the doctor, another Japanese, who was putting away his instruments.

"How do you feel, Mr. —?" he asked.

"Queasy," I said.

"No wonder," the doctor said. "Tomiko told us that he hit you with a rather large spanner."

I tried to sit up but discovered that I had been strapped down to the table. The doctor's aide started forward, until I slumped back.

"Is this necessary?" I asked. There was going to be hell to pay. I was going to have to let the captain in on what was happening aboard his ship.

"Under normal circumstances I'd say no," the doctor answered, looking at me with curiosity. "I mean if you were an ordinary stowaway. But you were armed, and after what the captain told us he found, I'd be surprised if you weren't shot and thrown overboard."

He turned and went across the dispensary to a desk where he picked up a telephone.

What the hell had they found? Whatever it was I had a sneaking suspicion it had something to do with Sharon Neumann.

"I'm finished with him down here," the doctor said in Japanese. A moment later he added, "Yes, sir. I'll have Sakai bring him up."

He hung up the phone, returned to the table on which I was strapped, and started undoing the restraints. "A word of advice, Mr. Whoever You Are, Sakai here is a very strong, surprisingly quick man. He could quite easily kill you with one hand. At home, before he joined the Merchant Marine, he was called the Terrible One for his karate prowess. He was finally kicked out of the amateur league after two opponents died because of his inability to show restraint. Do I make myself clear?"

"Perfectly," I said.

The doctor helped me sit up, a wave of dizziness and nausea washing over me, then helped me step down from the tall examining table and across the room where I was given a set of dungarees and deck shoes.

"May be a little small for you, but they were the largest size we could come up with."

I struggled into the clothes that were a bit short in the arms and legs, but loose enough at the shoulders and middle, and then Sakai herded me toward the door.

"Thanks for the patchup, doc," I said.

The doctor chuckled. "Behave yourself with the captain and I may not have to sew you up again. He is a man of extraordinary temper."

We went down a wide companionway that ran the width of the ship and then up three flights of stairs to the uppermost deck. The bridge was to the right, but Sakai motioned me toward the left, where at a highly polished wooden door he knocked once, and then opened it, letting me enter first.

The captain was a short, husky man, almost the twin of my guard. He stood behind a large desk. Across from him were three other men, all of them with stern expressions on their faces.

"That will be all," the captain said in Japanese, his voice harsh and guttural.

Sakai bowed, then went back out into the companionway, softly closing the door behind him.

For a long while the captain glared at me. "Why

do you want to destroy my ship?" he finally asked.

"I don't," I said.

The captain slammed his right fist on the desk top. "Do not lie to me!" he screamed. "We have found your bomb in the engine room. How did you place it there? Who are you?"

So that was it. Sharon had placed a bomb aboard. But what could she be thinking? If the *Akai Maru* went to the bottom with the strontium 90 aboard, it would be a major international disaster. As desperate as the Israelis were about the missing beta canister, I could not believe they would go to such lengths to get rid of it.

"I did not put a bomb aboard your ship, captain," I said stepping forward.

One of his officers leaped to his feet, a pistol in his hand, leveled at my gut. "Stop!" he shouted wildly.

I stood stock still. The man was young and obviously inexperienced with weapons. I did not want him to shoot me in a fit of nervousness.

"I mean you no harm, captain. Not you or your ship."

"Then what are you doing aboard? With weapons?"

"If you'll let me explain—" I started to say, when an ear-splitting explosion somewhere overhead, rocked the ship, sending us all sprawling to the deck.

The young officer with the pistol had fallen toward me. I quickly scrambled over to him and grabbed the gun from where he had dropped it, then shuffled backward out of his reach.

If Sharon was starting to blow up the ship, I was going to have to stop her.

The captain was on the phone, shouting something about damage control, and a siren was wailing out in the companionway.

"I don't want to hurt any of you," I said urgently as I backed up to the door. "I did not set any bombs aboard this ship."

The captain stood holding the phone to his ear, staring open mouthed at me. His three officers had gotten back on their feet and I could see by the look in their eyes that they were about ready to rush me.

I yanked open the door and stepped out into the companionway; the siren was so loud it blotted out all other sounds. Suddenly the gun was knocked out of my hand, and I was thrown at least ten feet away.

I rolled to the left, a sneaker-shod foot just missing my ribs, and I jumped to my feet as Sakai in the classic karate stance came after me.

The captain and his three officers burst from his cabin in a dead run, shouting something about the radio room. The motion distracted Sakai for just a split second, allowing me to leap up and catch him in the chest with both feet.

The captain and his officers were hurrying down the companionway, apparently not concerned about Sakai's ability to handle me. They needn't have worried. The man went down, but came up as if he had merely lost his balance momentarily and nothing more.

There was no way possible I was going to win a fair, hand-to-hand combat with this man. I feinted to the left, and as he stepped that way, I swiveled and took off down the corridor.

The doctor and two other men were just coming up the stairs as I raced around the corner. I managed to sidestep them and start down. The doctor shouted something at me, but then Sakai came around the corner from the companionway at full tilt and collided with all three men. They went down in a tumble of arms and legs and curses.

I was certain that Sharon would not have remained in the forecastle compartment. No doubt once I had been brought up to the dispensary the captain had ordered a thorough search of the bow area. If they had found the girl or any of our equipment, the captain would have mentioned it.

But where could she have gone, and why had she blown up the radio room? It would be impossible for me to find her aboard this mammoth ship unless she had left me some kind of a message or clue back down in the forecastle compartment.

I burst out of the stairwell, seven decks down, onto the main level companionway as a half a dozen crewmen all carrying wrecking bars and torches came up from below decks.

"The radio room," I shouted in Japanese. "The captain needs you on the double!"

To a seaman an order is an order, and it does not matter who it comes from; it is to be obeyed instantly, and if there are any questions, they come later.

Without hesitation the crewmen scrambled up the stairs, and I headed down the companionway to the portside main hatch which would take me outside.

Earlier I had noticed that the ship was equipped with battery-driven lanterns set on brackets at regular intervals along the companionways. In case of power failures they would provide light for the crew.

At the portside hatch I grabbed one of the lanterns from its bracket, ripping the short wire from the bulkhead, and it came on as I undogged the hatch and stepped outside.

It was cold, the wind was stiff and the seas looked rough. Above, the sky was dark, although I was sure it couldn't be much past 9:30 or 10:00 A.M. We were in for a storm. And by the looks of the weather it was going to be a good one.

No one was on the main deck as I hurried away from the superstructure and headed forward across what looked like a combination football field and Texas oil field.

Partway forward, I slipped on a patch of grease at the same moment the ship lurched, and I was thrown to my hands and knees, the lantern clattering toward one of the wide scuppers. I lunged out catching it just before it went overboard, and a moment later I was back on my feet and continuing forward.

The ship was plowing now through the rising waves and it would not be long before any movement above decks near the bow would be impossible. Already a fine spray was breaking forward every time the ship rode heavily into a trough.

It took me nearly ten minutes to make it all the way to the maintenance hatch, and here the motion of the ship was very rough as she worked her way through the building waves.

Before I opened the hatch I looked back. A huge black hole had been torn from the top level of the superstructure and the antennas located there were either completely gone, or down and twisted. Even the radar dish was bent nearly double and lay over on its side.

No one had come after me yet, but I knew it would not take them very long to figure out where I was heading. I was going to have to hurry.

I flung the hatch open, climbed down to the platform and pulled the heavy metal lid closed again, redogging the latch.

Immediately I started down the ladder, the going very awkward because I had to hold onto the bulky lantern and because of the increasingly violent motions of the ship.

Twice I nearly lost my grip, but I did not slow down. I had to find the Israeli woman and stop her from sinking the ship. The one fact she was not aware of, was that the strontium 90 was no longer encased in its beta canister. It had been taken out of the heavy lead container, and I was sure it was now mixed with the five million gallons of crude oil in the ship's hold. I still had no idea why the Russians wanted to send contaminated oil to the States, but if the ship went down and the oil was spilled, it would be a hundred years or more before the Atlantic Ocean recovered. If it ever would.

Finally at the bottom, I shined the lantern's beam toward the pipeline room, on the other side of which was the forecastle compartment hatch, and listened, straining every sense to detect the presence of someone else down there. But I could hear nothing other than the thrumming of the engines a thousand feet aft and the bow plates crashing against the seas.

Carefully I moved across the L-Deck catwalk, entered the pipeline room and approached the forecastle compartment hatch.

Again I stopped to listen, but still nothing seemed out of the ordinary, so I unlatched the hatch, pulled it open and shined my light inside.

Nothing was changed. The anchor chain, plates and stacks of wooden crates were in the same positions they had been in before. I stepped inside, crossed the compartment and went around the stack of boxes to where Sharon had stowed her gear, but there was nothing there. She had taken everything with her.

I turned and shined my light over to where I had laid my backpack, but it was gone as well.

Working quickly then, I searched the entire compartment looking for some kind of a message or clue that would tell me where she had gone, but there was nothing.

I was stuck now. Without weapons. Without proper clothing, and without the Geiger counter and radio. I also realized that I was hungry. I hadn't eaten since early yesterday evening aboard the submarine.

After the explosion in the radio room, which had wiped out the ship's communications and radar facilities, I was sure the captain would not listen to anything I would have to say to him. And without communications there would be no way for me to prove that I was telling the truth.

I tried to think. Tried to put myself in Sharon's shoes. She had watched them take me away. She knew they would be coming back to search this compartment. So where would she have gone?

Somewhere aft, I suspected. If she was going to sink the ship she would have to be somewhere near the lifeboats which were located near the living sections of the ship.

There was no other choice for me, I thought glumly, except to go aft and somehow find her.

I had laid the lantern on the crates across the compartment from me, and I turned to go back and get it. Sakai was standing just within the doorway, a slight, malevolent grin on his face.

"I don't want to fight with you," I said once I got over my initial shock. I took a step to the right toward the crates. He matched my move. "I mean you no harm."

We were about ten feet apart, the crates less than five feet from me. He took a step my way and I moved closer to the wooden boxes. If I could get him tangled up behind the crates I might be able to make it to the hatch and somehow jam the lock from the outside.

"I didn't set the bombs aboard this ship," I said, edging closer to the crates. "As a matter of fact I'm trying to stop them."

Sakai lunged at me then, moving with incredible speed and agility, his right hand swinging around.

I jumped backward, stumbling over the nearest crate and falling to the other side at the same instant Sakai's jackhammer blow just missed my neck, his powerful hand crashing instead into the top of the crate.

The thick wooden lid splintered and the entire box fell apart, spilling anchor chain links down on me. They were at least six inches in diameter, made out of one inch bar stock, each one weighing at least ten pounds.

I grabbed one of the links and rolled over twice, then jumped to my feet as Sakai shoved the remains of the crate aside as if it was nothing more than a toy, and came after me.

I backed up a step, brought my right arm back and threw the chain link with every ounce of strength I had, hitting the man squarely in the forehead. His head rocked back, and for a terrible moment I thought he would shrug off even that blow; but then he shook his head, looked at me with a confused expression and sunk to his knees.

Around the crates I scooped up the lantern from where it had been knocked to the deck and raced to the open hatch where I stopped and turned back.

The man had been doing his job. He was defending his ship, nothing more. He was not involved with the strontium 90, neither was the captain or most of the crew. Only the two Red Fist of November terrorists who had signed on as ordinary seamen were involved in this thing.

There was a very good chance that Sakai would die if I left him here. And yet to help him back to the dispensary could mean my death warrant, if not at the hands of the captain who believed I had blown up his radio room, then at the hands of one of the Red Fist crewmen.

For a moment I could not make the decision, torn between the bombs, and the man here. But then I finally realized there was no real choice. I sighed deeply and went back into the compartment where the stocky little man was still on his knees staring up at me, a dazed expression in his eyes, a huge welt forming on his forehead.

I put the lantern down on one of the crates and helped Sakai to his feet, putting his left arm around my neck so that I could support his weight. Then, with my free hand, I grabbed the lantern and struggled with the nearly unconscious man to the hatch and out into the pipeline room.

There was no way I would be able to get the man up the sixty-foot ladder to the bow deck, especially

not now with the ship smashing through the heavy
seas the way she was.

My only other option was to drag him along the
length of the ship through one of the maintenance
tunnels and into the engine room area. From there
I could get him up to the dispensary.

Across the pipeline room I came onto the L-
Deck catwalk, turned to the right and started toward one of the tunnels when something hard
crashed into the back of my head and I was out.

I had vague recollections of being carried somewhere very dark, the smell of crude oil strong;
some time after that I was in a room with bright
lights. Finally I knew I was in bed and I let myself
drift to escape the terrible headache that throbbed
every time my heart beat.

For awhile I had a clear vision of the woman and
two men dead in the apartment in Kuwait City,
their bodies gruesomely eaten half away by radiation poisoning. But then I dreamed I was on a
roller coaster that was moving up and down the
tracks at ever-increasing speeds, the wind shrieking
around me.

Finally, I opened my eyes and stared up at the
featureless metal ceiling as I mentally explored my
body for any massive damage.

The ship was lurching and heaving, and from
outside I could hear the wind shrieking and howling around the superstructure. We were in the
middle of the storm that had been building when I
escaped back to the forecastle compartment.

I sat up, the motion causing my head to nearly
explode, bringing tears to my eyes and making my

stomach flop. After several long seconds the feeling passed and the pain at the back of my skull was reduced to a dull throbbing.

A small light had been left on over a tiny desk across the room from me. I turned toward it as I flipped the covers back and swung my legs over the edge of the narrow cot I had been laying on. Carefully I got to my feet, reaching out with my left hand to brace myself against the bulkhead.

I was in a small cabin, furnished with the bunk, the desk, a couple of shelves with curtains across them and a narrow closet. A photograph of a young woman dressed in a flowered kimono and holding a small baby, was hung on the wall over the desk. The curtains covering the closet opening were half parted, revealing several neatly hung uniforms. They had put me up in one of the junior officer's cabins.

There was a small clock on the desk and I struggled across the room to it, having some trouble focusing my eyes and making my legs work. I was reasonably certain that I was suffering from a minor concussion. I just hoped that the effects of two severe blows on my head would pass, so that I would be able to operate normally.

At the desk I picked up the clock and studied it for a long moment, the positions of the hands not making any sense to me at first. But then it was as if a fog had been lifted from my brain, and I realized it was four thirty. Instinctively I looked over at the porthole; it was pitch black outside. It was four-thirty in the morning.

I was still dressed in the dungarees; my deck shoes were laying beside the cot. I went back across the cabin, sat down on the bed and pulled on the shoes.

As I was tying the second lace, I could hear that someone was out in the companionway. I looked up as the door swung open and a bright light shined directly in my eyes.

"Get up," a man's voice, with an odd, almost French accent ordered.

"What's going on?" I asked, trying to shield my eyes with my right hand.

I heard the unmistakable click of a pistol's hammer being cocked. "Get up, or I will kill you here and now," the man said.

Lebanese. His accent was Lebanese. Red Fist of November. It all came into focus at once, and I got unsteadily to my feet.

"Why did your people steal the strontium 90?" I asked. My voice sounded weak even to me.

"Move," the man snapped.

I could not make out his face because of the strong light in my eyes, but I could see that he was a short man, not much larger than most of the Japanese aboard.

"Your friends in Kuwait are dead, you know," I said. "Radiation poisoning."

The man said nothing, the light did not waver.

"The KGB killed your friends in Beirut. I saw it happen."

"We're going to step out into the companionway and you're going to turn to the right and go outside from the starboard hatch. Make any kind of a funny move and I will kill you instantly."

I had absolutely no chance of disarming the man in these close quarters, and although I knew he meant to kill me, I was going to have to go along with him at least for the moment.

He moved back out into the companionway and I followed him, turning right down the corridor as he had instructed.

"Move," he ordered again, and I started toward the starboard side hatch about fifty feet away.

"I know that the strontium 90 was probably placed in the oil," I said. "But why?"

"Shut up," the man snapped.

"It'll never get to the States. This ship has been rigged with bombs. One of them blew out the radio room. Another is in the engine room."

"I know," the man laughed. "I put them there."

"You?" I said, and I started to turn around.

"Get going—or I'll kill you here and now!"

I turned back and shuffled the rest of the way to the hatch, which I undogged and shoved open. It was raining and the wind howled like a wounded, enraged beast, engulfing us both as we stepped out onto the starboard deck, the rail five feet away. The sea was wild, the waves mammoth, at times nearly as high as the sixty-foot bow.

"You're going overboard," the man said.

I turned around. "No, wait."

"Either jump and take your chances, or I'll shoot you now and throw you overboard myself."

NINE

"How about a life jacket?" I asked, glancing over the rail at the sea more than fifty feet below. If I could distract him for just a moment I figured I could rush him.

He laughed. "Over the rail," he said, starting to raise his pistol.

I moved to the left, expecting the shot at any moment, when the man grunted, his eyes went wide and he fell on his face at my feet, the handle of a knife protruding from his back.

Sharon Neumann materialized from the darkness fifteen feet aft, a grim expression on her face. I was never so glad to see anyone in my life.

"Are you all right?" she asked.

"I'm just fine now."

She bent down over the body, pulled her knife out, wiped it off on the man's jacket and sheathed it at her side. Next, she flipped the man over on his side, and while steadying his body in that position with one hand, she opened his jacket with the other and pulled his shirt up, revealing a small black figure tattooed beneath his left breast.

"Red Fist of November," she said, looking up at me.

I recognized the man's face, now, from the photos Hawk had brought over from AXE archives.

"One down one to go," I said.

Careful to keep the body facedown so that no blood would spill on the deck, we heaved it up over the rail and let it go.

"They blew the radio room," I told her. "And there's at least one other bomb in the engine room."

"I know," the woman replied. "I've found two alongside the main tanks. They're equipped with negative pressure fuses as well as radio detonators. Move the bombs and they blow." She stepped across the deck and looked through the porthole in the hatch.

"Where'd you move our things?" I asked. It would be dawn soon and we would have to stay out of sight until nightfall.

"The stuffing box compartment. It's below and aft of the engine room where the main shaft passes through the hull and connects with the propeller."

"We'd better get moving before the day crew comes on," I suggested.

She turned without a word and hurried aft. As far as I could remember from the ship's blueprints I had studied, the only way down to the stuffing box compartment, was directly through the engine room. Unless Sharon had found another way down there I couldn't see how we would make it. There was always a crew on duty down there.

She stopped at a hatch almost all the way aft, looked through a porthole, then undogged the hatch and we slipped inside.

We were in a wide companionway, and she

pointed toward the opposite end at the same moment I heard several men laughing.

"Galley and crew's mess," she whispered.

I nodded. The stairway down to the engine room was through a hatch immediately to our right, and Sharon opened it without hesitation and started down. I closed the hatch softly behind me and followed her, the throbbing sounds of the huge diesel engines below us very loud in the confined stairwell.

At least three decks down Sharon pulled up short and motioned for me to stop and be quiet. I stood there, holding my breath, and then I heard it. Someone was coming up the stairs.

I came down to Sharon's level and pulled her off the stairwell onto a narrow catwalk that snaked its way through a maze of pipes and other machinery, until we were several feet from the stairs crouching down in the shadows.

A couple of minutes later two men came up the stairs, passed our hiding spot and continued up. Sharon started to move, but I held her back. A moment later a third man passed our position and continued up.

We worked our way back to the stairs and continued down four more decks to a wide companionway with a very high ceiling. The decking underfoot was made up of sections of grating, below which I could see a maze of pipelines and other machinery.

About fifty feet down the companionway a wide doorway in the forward bulkhead was open and there was light shining from it. Sharon pointed toward it. "The engine room is through there," she said. "We've got to get past the hatch."

I nodded and followed her down the companionway. She stopped at the opening and peered inside. A moment later she quickly stepped past it and then pointed down.

At the opening I looked inside. The engine room deck itself was about twenty feet below, the huge diesels rising even higher than the deck on which I was standing.

A half a dozen men were engaged in a conversation directly in front of one of the engines, their backs turned our way, so I quickly stepped across the opening, joining Sharon on the other side.

There was no way we would be able to get across the engine room. Not with those men down there, and I told her as much.

"I found another way," she said, leading me another fifty feet down the companionway where she dropped to her knees and pulled up a four-foot-by-four-foot section of the floor grating.

I held it for her and she jumped down through the opening. A moment later I followed her, finding myself on a narrow catwalk four feet beneath the level of the floor.

When I had the grating in place above us, Sharon headed back toward the engine room opening, moving softly in a hunched-over scramble.

Just past the opening, Sharon stiffened and stopped in her tracks. A moment later a man emerged from the stairway and came down the companionway directly over our heads, went through the engine room hatch, and climbed down.

When he was gone, Sharon continued along the cramped passageway until we came to a ladder well. She started down into the darkness and I followed.

About thirty feet down I heard a soft splash, and

then a light came on and I looked down. Sharon had stepped away from the ladder and was standing in water nearly to her knees, a flashlight in her right hand.

I joined her a moment later, the water ice cold. "The bilge?" I asked softly.

She nodded. "We're at the lowest point in the ship here. The stuffing box compartment is on the other side of the engine room, and one deck up."

"After you," I said. The exertions of the past twenty minutes had caused my headache to come back and I felt slightly lightheaded and nauseous. Just a little farther, I told myself, and I would be able to rest.

She turned and splashed through the water, her light bobbing and shining as she climbed over wide steel beams that formed, I supposed, the internal bracing ribs of the vessel.

We went at least seventy-five feet aft, when Sharon stopped, shined her light overhead, went a few feet farther, then reached up and shoved open a hatch. A second later she had climbed up out of the bilge.

"Come on," she said from above, and I made it to the open hatch, reached up and climbed into the stuffing box room directly beneath the spinning shaft that gleamed wetly in the dim light.

The noise here was not quite as loud as I expected it would be, but the tiny compartment was cold and damp. It was not going to be a particularly comfortable day.

Sharon went across the compartment and climbed up a ladder to the ceiling about eight feet up as I closed the bilge hatch and then went over to her.

She had jammed the hatch—which led, I presumed, up to the engine room—with a short wrecking bar which she had picked up from somewhere, and when she came back down from the ladder she seemed satisfied. "It hasn't moved," she said. "Which means no one has been down here since I left."

She shined her light over to a corner on the far side of the compartment from the spinning shaft. Both sleeping bags were laid out side by side. On my bag was the contents of my backpack, minus my radio and the Uzo submachinegun.

"What'd you do with the radio?" I asked.

"Threw it overboard," she said. "This is an Israeli operation. I don't want your people interfering with it."

From what I had been able to see from the bow, the radio room had been totally destroyed. If she had actually thrown my radio overboard, it left only her radio as a means of communications from this ship.

"Is there a gunboat out there?" I asked. "Is that who you're in contact with?"

There was a roaring sound in my ears above and beyond the noise of the rotating propeller shaft, and the heavy throb of the engines above us. I felt curiously detached from everything, almost as if I was sitting on my own shoulder watching myself and the woman. And yet I knew that I was going to have to do something, not only to stop the Red Fist of November terrorist still aboard who had placed bombs on the ship, but this woman as well.

"I told you—" Sharon began, but I waved her answer off.

My arm suddenly seemed leaden. Every movement I made took a supreme effort. I knew that I could not go on much longer without rest.

"You can't recover the strontium 90," I told her. "It's in the oil."

"I know that," she said, her voice hollow. "They dumped it in the tanks before we left Kuwait. I'm sure of it."

"Then what are your orders?"

"Find the Red Fist of November people and kill them," she said.

"Then what?"

"Either stop this ship from going to the United States or destroy it."

"No," I said stepping forward. "You don't understand." I stumbled and fell to my knees, the roaring coming even louder in my ears.

Sharon was at my side. "What is it?" she said from a long way off. "What's the matter?"

I looked up at her and tried to shake my head. "No," I said, my voice weak. I wasn't sure if she had heard me, but I had to make her understand that the strontium 90 was no longer in its beta canister. The terrorists had somehow dumped it directly into the oil. The entire five million gallons of crude aboard this ship was contaminated.

But then I was laying on the deck, my cheek against the cold metal, and I could feel her fingers exploring the two wounds on the back of my head. She was saying something but I could make no sense of it.

She dragged me across the deck and laid me on my sleeping bag. I was aware of that much. And she was undressing me, the cold suddenly making me shiver violently.

I awoke sometime later—hours or minutes I couldn't tell—and for a long moment I lay in my sleeping bag, listening to the sounds of the ship and mentally cataloguing my own condition. My mouth was foul, every muscle in my body ached and my head felt as if it had been run through a meat grinder.

It was pitch black in the tiny compartment and very cold. Even in the sleeping bag I was shivering, due in part, I was sure, to my condition.

"Sharon?" I called softly, but there was no answer. I struggled up to a sitting position. "Sharon?" I called again, but still the only sounds in the compartment were the spinning propeller shaft and the engines above.

I unzipped the sleeping bag and crawled out of it, almost immediately bumping into a backpack. Opening it I found a flashlight, which I flipped on.

Sharon was gone. The metal bar was still jammed in the hatch lock mechanism overhead and the hatch which led down into the bilge was closed. I had no idea what time it was, but I was reasonably certain I had not been out for the entire day. So where was she?

Her pack lay on top of her sleeping bag a couple of feet away from me. I crawled over to it on my hands and knees, alarmed at how weak I still was. I fumbled with the straps, finally getting the pack open. From within, I drew out her Geiger counter, a high-frequency radio and another small device that had a series of switches on its front panel, along with a key lock mechanism and a short telescoping antenna.

For a long moment I looked at the device wondering what in hell it was, but suddenly it struck me and I shivered involuntarily. It was a detonator. Sharon had evidently placed her own explosives aboard this ship and intended to sink it. Evidently she was counting on the idea that the strontium 90 was still safely encased in its beta canister.

They were going to risk an oil spill to get rid of the radioactive material. Perhaps later they planned on recovering the canister with a bathyscaphe.

I stared down at the detonator and radio, the cold penetrating deep inside me again. No matter what the consequences I could not allow that to happen. I had to stop those bombs from going off.

The back cover of the detonating unit was held in place by a half a dozen Philips head screws. I laid it on the sleeping bag near the radio and dumped the contents of Sharon's backpack alongside the units.

In the pile of items, which included her clothing as well as my submachine gun and spare clips, was a small tool kit. I took a Philips head screwdriver out, and within a couple of minutes had the back off the detonator, and had removed its two batteries. Then I yanked out as many wires and components as I could and smashed the rest with the handle of the screwdriver. There would be no way she could fix it now.

Next I turned my attention to the radio. If there was a gunboat standing by out there somewhere, she could radio it and ask for help sinking the ship. Destroying the radio would cut off my line of communications as well, but I could not take the chance that she would call for help. I took it apart and yanked out most of its components, making it totally irreparable.

The roaring sound was coming back to me and my head throbbed as I screwed the back plates on the detonator and radio and then replaced both pieces of equipment in Sharon's backpack.

Next I scooped up all the smashed components I had removed from her gear and carried them over to the bilge hatch which I opened, and then threw the things down into the water.

If she didn't take the equipment apart she would never know that they had been wrecked until she needed to use them. By then, I hoped, crawling back to my sleeping bag, it would be too late.

I was shivering more violently than ever as I pulled the sleeping bag cover up around my neck and let myself go, gratefully into unconsciousness.

Some time later I became aware of something warm and incredibly soft laying against me. For a long while I had difficulty in making my brain work, until I suddenly realized that Sharon was back and in the sleeping bag with me. She was nude, her arms and legs around me, holding me tightly, her breasts crushed against my chest.

It was pitch black, and for several minutes I was content to lay still, enjoying the warmth of her body. I felt much better. Most of the pain was gone, and although I was weak and very hungry, I was sure I was recovering from the blows on my head.

Finally I raised my right hand out of the sleeping bag and caressed her cheek. She stiffened instantly.

"You're awake," she said, her voice soft just inches from my ear.

"How long have I been out?" I asked.

"Most of the day." She started to pull away, but I dropped my right arm around her shoulder and held her close.

"Don't," I said.

She struggled for a moment, but then lay still. "You were cold. This was the only way I knew of keeping you warm. How do you feel now?"

"Much better," I said, and I kissed her on the lips.

She pulled back at first, but then she responded, snuggling even closer and returning my kiss.

"I thought you were going to die on me," she said. "I was frightened."

I let my right hand run down her back and then gently across the delicate curves of her buttocks. She shivered.

The strontium 90, the Red Fist of November, the contaminated oil and her plans for this ship all seemed very far away, as I gently pushed her over on her back. She didn't fight me any longer as I caressed her breasts, the nipples already hard, and then let my fingertips wander across her flat stomach.

She raised up off the deck arching her hips, a soft moan escaping from her lips. Then I was on top of her, her legs wrapped tightly around my body and we were making love, gently and slowly, as I kissed her neck and breasts.

Afterward, when we had finally parted, she reached out in the darkness, fumbled with something for a moment, and then a match flared as she lit a cigarette. In the brief glow I could see that she was smiling, but there also was an intensely worried look in her eyes.

She took a drag from the cigarette and then passed it to me. I inhaled deeply, the smoke making me lightheaded for a few seconds.

"That was very nice," I said as we lay side by side in the warm sleeping bag.

She chuckled. "Are you finally warm?"

"For the moment. But I have a feeling I won't stay that way very long."

She laughed again and took the cigarette from me.

"Where did you go?" I asked softly.

She had started to bring the cigarette to her lips, but the tip stopped in midair. "What?"

"I woke up and you were gone," I said. "Where did you go? What were you doing?"

"I went up to the engine room companionway," she said after a long hesitation.

"Why?"

"I wanted to see if they were searching for you. They had to discover you were missing some time in the night."

"Are they?"

"I couldn't tell," she said in a small voice. I knew she was lying.

I reached up behind me and fumbled around her things that she had dumped beside us when she had gotten undressed, and found her flashlight.

"What are you doing—"

I sat up and switched on the light. "You're lying to me," I said sharply.

She sat up, the sleeping bag falling away, exposing her lovely breasts. She didn't seem to notice. Although the back of my head still throbbed, I was rested and my mind was no longer fuzzy. She glanced over toward her backpack.

"I found it," I said following her gaze. "And I know it's a detonator. How many bombs have you set up?"

She looked at me, a hard glint in her eyes. "I told you before, Nick, that this is an Israeli operation. I won't have you interfering with it. That's why I destroyed your radio."

"You mean to destroy this ship if you can't recover the strontium 90?"

She nodded. "Those are my orders."

"The strontium 90 was dumped in the holds."

"I believe it now," she said. "I took your Geiger counter and checked it out. I can't pinpoint the source, but I know it's in there."

"You don't understand, Sharon," I said. "The strontium 90 has been dumped into the oil. The strontium 90—not the beta canister."

Her eyes went wide. She started to say something, but then clamped it off.

"I found the beta canister with the Beersheba markings in an apartment in Kuwait City. It was empty."

"It's not true," she said.

"It is, Sharon. I was sent here to recover the material. Or to make sure this ship was not sunk. If there was an oil spill now, it would contaminate a very large hunk of this ocean for a very long time."

"If you knew the strontium 90 was no longer in its container, why did you think there was a possibility of recovering it?" she asked. There was a triumphant look in her eyes now.

"There was the off chance that they had put the material in another container," I said. "There were three people dead in the Dasma apartment, dead of radiation poisoning, which means they handled the stuff. I thought that there was a possibility they had transferred the strontium 90 into another lead-lined container, something that wouldn't look like a radioactive materials container. Maybe a lead-lined oil drum. They would have had to do it that way to get the stuff past dock security."

"Then we're back where we started," Sharon said. "The strontium 90 is in some other kind of container in the bottom of the hold."

I shook my head. "I had hoped that would be the case, but it isn't. You proved it yourself."

"I proved it—" she started to say, but then she stopped in mid-sentence. "My God," she said softly. "You're right. There's nothing wrong with my Geiger counter. Yours showed the same readings."

"That's right. Low level radiation everywhere near the holds."

"They actually dumped the stuff into the oil. But why?"

"I don't know," I had to admit. "But whatever their reasons, this ship is carrying five million gallons of radioactive crude to the refineries at Bakersfield, California."

"I've got six bombs in place," she said after a long time.

"And the Red Fist of November crewman put at least two aboard," I said. "Can we disconnect yours?"

She shook her head. "Pressure sensitive fuses," she said. "Just like the two others I found alongside the tanks."

"Then we've just got his to worry about," I said. "I destroyed your detonator so there's no chance yours will go off, even accidentally."

She got an odd expression on her face, but then she smiled. "I knew I should have taken it along with me," she said. "I underestimated you."

"Don't tell me you still intend to try to sink this ship?"

She shook her head. "Not after what you told

me. So it won't matter that you destroyed my detonator. At least not until three."

She started to climb out of the sleeping bag, but I reached out, grabbed her arm and yanked her back.

"Three?" I said, my stomach churning. "Have you set timers on them?"

"No," she said. "But you were right about another thing. There is one of our gunboats out there. They have their own detonator. If the bombs don't go off by three in the morning, then they'll blow them up. I'll radio the boat and explain the situation."

She must have read the stunned look on my face, because she paled. "Oh, no. Did you destroy my radio, too?"

TEN

Nude, Sharon Neumann was a very feminine woman, but dressing in black commando coveralls, her face darkened, the knife at her side, and a silenced pistol in a shoulder holster, had changed her entire manner. She was now a dedicated, tough and very capable Mossad agent.

It was shortly after six o'clock P.M. We had eaten a quick, tasteless meal of C rations, and now stood ready at the hatch to the bilge.

The wrecked radio room, we had figured, held our best option for the moment. There was a possibility of finding something usable up there. Even a small emergency locator beacon transmitter might work to somehow get a message to the gunboat.

"I can't believe that your orders included killing the captain and the crew," I said. It bothered me. The Israelis were tough, but they were not murderers of innocent people.

Sharon had just bent down to undog the hatch, but she stood up again. "Good God, what do you take us for?"

"You did place some explosives aboard, and you were carrying a detonator," I said.

"That's right," she admitted. "We were planning on sinking this ship. But only after we had gotten the captain and crew off safely. We were then going to retrieve the beta canister from the ocean floor."

"How were you supposed to get the captain and crew off this ship?"

"Let them find the bombs, let myself be caught and admit I was a terrorist."

"You would have been running a hell of a risk that one of the Red Fist crewmen would kill you."

"I was supposed to find and kill them first."

"Then your gunboat would just happen to show up and pick up the crew," I said.

"Exactly," she nodded.

It still didn't make much sense. "Then there's nothing to worry about," I said. "The gunboat captain won't blow this ship anyway."

"He might, Nick, if he doesn't hear from me by three o'clock A.M. In that event he's to assume I'm dead, in which case he'd radio the *Akai Maru* to abandon ship."

"But he can't radio now."

"No."

"He wouldn't destroy this ship without warning the crew."

"I don't know," she said, a troubled expression in her eyes. "We never expected your presence, nor did we suspect that the Red Fist crewmen would have placed their own bombs. It's my guess that our gunboat will approach the *Akai Maru* and send a light signal to abandon ship."

"If that happens," I said, "the terrorist will blow the ship."

"Exactly. Which is why we've got to get a message to my people to stand off, at least until we can approach the captain and explain everything to him."

Approaching the captain would probably do little or nothing for us, I thought. The man was convinced that it was I who had planted the bombs aboard his ship and had blown up his radio room. If there had been anyone on duty up there, and I suspected there had been, they would have been killed. Also I had nearly killed Sakai, and in the captain's eyes I was most likely the one behind the disappearance of the crewman whose body Sharon and I had dumped over the rail. The captain would be in no mood to listen to my story.

I had not told Sharon about the *Whiteshark* shadowing us, but I was reasonably certain that the submarine had detected the presence of the Israeli gunboat. What Farmington would do with that knowledge, however, or how he was taking my radio silence was another question for which I had no answer at the moment.

Low key, Hawk had told me from the very beginning. But this mission had been anything but that. And now any overt action by Sharon and I, by the gunboat, or by the *Whiteshark* would surely force the terrorist into detonating his bombs.

I was dressed in my own clothes now, from the spares I had carried in my pack. The Uzo submachine gun was strapped to my back and several of my zippered pockets contained spare clips of ammunition that I hoped I would never have to use.

"Let's go then," I said to Sharon.

"I'm sorry that this had to happen," she apologized.

I thought about the Russians in Beirut and Hawk's suspicion that this was the operation of a man named Kobelev back in Moscow. There was a lot she did not know. But at this point it didn't matter how the situation had evolved, we were in it now up to our necks. Together.

Sharon bent down to the hatch again, undogged it and pulled it open. She flipped on her flashlight and then crawled down into the bilge. I turned off the lantern that we had used for light in the stuffing box compartment, then crawled down into the bilge behind her after closing the hatch, and we headed forward toward the engine room companionway, the water ice cold and foul smelling.

When we reached the ladder that would take us up, Sharon stopped until I caught up with her. A dim light filtered down to us from the companionway thirty feet above.

"The crew change should already have taken place—" she started to say, but I shook my head.

"It's too dangerous that way. Anyone coming to or from the engine room could run into us," I said. I remembered from the ship's blueprints that there were a number of access tunnels from the bilge up to the deck, the ladder running between the outer wall of the holds and the inner wall of the hull itself. The tunnels were used for emergency pumping of the bilges.

"You don't mean to try the pumping wells?"

I nodded. "We can get to the radio room from the outside that way. Less chance of being spotted."

She shook her head. "There's a storm out there. We'd be swept off the deck."

"It's a chance we're going to have to take," I said. "If we're spotted by the crew and the terrorist finds out, he'll blow the bombs."

For several long seconds she seemed to weigh the

logic of my argument. "You're right," she agreed finally, and she turned away from the ladder and continued forward.

The nearest access hatch, from what I could re- member of the diagrams, was located about a hun- dred feet forward of the superstructure and led di- rectly onto the deck between one of the loading ports. That meant we'd have to cross a hundred feet of open deck, climb up to the top level of the crew's quarters and then into the radio room from the blasted away opening.

It would not be easy under any circumstances, but with the storm raging outside it would be in- teresting.

The farther forward we went, however, the more violent the ship's motion became from the storm and the less certain I became of our chances of suc- cess topside.

Sharon felt the same way, because at one point she stopped and turned back to me. "We'll never make it this way, Nick."

"We've got to try," I said. If we went the other way and did run into one of the crewmen, we would have to stop him. I did not relish the idea of killing innocent men, no matter how critical the mission was.

I could see that she understood exactly what I was saying, and why I was saying it, and she finally shrugged her shoulders, turned around and contin- ued forward. About ten feet farther, however, she let out a little cry and rushed ahead.

"What is it?" I called out, racing after her.

She stopped just past one of the hull ribs and was shining the beam of her flashlight on a lumpy gray mass that was attached to the hold plates, about chest high.

I climbed over the rib and joined her. "What'd you find—" I started to ask again, but then I recognized the thing on the bulkhead. It was a bomb with enough plastique to blow a hole twenty feet in diameter not only through the hold plates, but through the hull as well.

"One of yours?" I asked.

She looked up at me and shook her head. "No."

I took the flashlight from her and closely examined the bomb. A small detonator device was attached to the middle of the lump of plastique, a tiny receiving antenna sticking about two inches out of it. A second set of wires was looped around behind the plastique, connected no doubt to some kind of a pressure sensitive switch. If we attempted to move the bomb, or in any way tamper with it, the thing would blow. Simple, but very deadly.

Actually seeing one of the bombs down here against the hold plates made me very conscious of the delicate situation we were in. At any moment the terrorist could decide to set this and the other bombs off. The tiniest thing could spook him.

I shined the light forward, down the passageway, and without a word Sharon and I continued toward the pumping tunnel that would lead up to the open deck.

A hundred feet later we found another of the obscene-looking bombs attached to the hold plates, and a hundred feet beyond that still another.

"He's got the entire ship rigged to blow," Sharon said, the awe obvious in her voice.

"He sets these off and no one would have a chance of getting off before she sank to the bottom. Not even if you were topside on the open deck in a calm sea."

"But why?" Sharon asked. "I don't understand what they're doing. Are they trying to get contaminated oil to the States? Or are they planning on dumping the oil in the ocean?"

"I don't know," I said. "It doesn't make any sense to me either."

A short distance beyond this last bomb, we came to the ladder that led sixty feet straight up to the deck hatch.

I started up immediately, and when I got about ten feet, Sharon directly beneath me, I stopped a moment and looked down at her.

"It's too hard to climb with the flashlight in one hand. I'm going to switch it off and put it in my pocket. We'll go the rest of the way by feel. Be careful."

She looked up at me, her eyes wide, and she nodded. "You too," she said.

I switched the flashlight off, plunging us into total darkness, stuffed it in one of my pockets, and then very slowly and carefully continued up the ladder one rung at a time, making sure with each step that I had a firm grip before I moved up another.

The rungs of the ladder were cold and slippery, and the radical motions of the ship through the storm-driven sea made the going extremely difficult.

Twice Sharon asked me to stop; she had to rest. And both times I pulled out the flashlight and switched it on. The light gave both of us some comfort.

It took at least a half an hour to make it up to the catwalk that was just seven or eight feet below the hatch itself, where I again turned on the flashlight.

Sharon joined me on the cramped platform where we rested for a full five minutes.

"The easy part is over," I commented.

She managed a slight smile. "I know," she said. She looked at her watch. "It's almost seven."

"Eight hours," I said. "It doesn't leave us much time."

She looked up at the hatch. From here we could hear the wind howling outside, and we had to hang on to the low rail that ringed the platform as the ship plunged through the waves.

"Are you ready?" I asked.

She nodded, then leaned forward and kissed me. "I'm glad you're here."

I climbed the last section of the ladder, undogged the hatch and started to shove it open when the wind caught it, tearing it out of my hands and slamming it open on the deck with a reverberating clang.

Instantly we were engulfed in the wind and rain that was so loud it made any talk totally impossible.

I hauled myself up over the lip of the opening and out onto the heaving deck. It was pitch black outside, and the only thing I could see of the superstructure a hundred feet aft was the vague glimmer of a light from one of the windows.

Sharon came up out of the pumping tunnel and I helped her over the edge. It took both of us to get the hatch closed again, and for a long minute we lay on the deck, hanging onto a valve handle. She shouted something at me, but even though we were only two feet apart, her voice was lost to the wind, and I shook my head and pointed to the rear.

She nodded and we left the comparative safety of the hatch and started aft, crawling on our hands and knees from one handhold to the next.

It was very cold, and within seconds I was soaked to the skin, my hands numb, my world reduced to a small section of the deck plating directly in front of me.

Every now and then I looked back, and each time Sharon smiled at me, although I could see she was having a tough time of it.

Sometime later, I had no idea how long it was, we made it to the superstructure, a few feet to the left of one of the doors. The wind was coming directly on the bow, so the eight-story tall living section of the ship offered us absolutely no protection from the storm.

Sharon pointed to the left, and after we had rested for a few moments, I headed that way, still on my hands and knees, finally coming to the ladder that rose up eighty feet from the main deck.

Far above us I could hear an occasional sharp crack, like gunfire, and after a moment I realized that the crew must have covered the opening to the radio room with a tarp, and I was hearing the flapping of the canvas in the gale.

I had stood up and was hanging onto the ladder, when Sharon got to her feet beside me and I motioned to her that I wanted her knife.

She pulled it out of its sheath and handed it over. I stuck it in my belt and started up the ladder, the wind and rain tearing at my body, making each step difficult and very dangerous.

I stopped a few feet up to make sure Sharon was doing all right, and again she smiled up at me, and I continued, one rung at a time.

The farther up I climbed the louder the cracking of the canvas became, so that at times I was sure we were nearly there. But the ladder seemed to go up forever, the wind building in intensity.

Twice I almost lost my grip, my heart pounding nearly out of my chest, but both times I managed somehow to hang on with fingers that had long since lost any feeling. Yet Sharon was always just below me with a smile whenever I looked down.

And then we were there, the canvas flapping wildly in the wind, one of the downed antennas less than two feet to the right.

The explosion had blown the front of the radio room completely out and had torn a large hole in the roof. The ship's crew had tied a large piece of canvas over the opening and it had come loose on the opposite side of the opening from where I was perched on the ladder.

I pulled the knife from my belt and, hanging on with my left hand, reached out and made a long slit in the material that immediately tore all the way to the roof, the edges snapping like high-powered rifle shots.

I stuck the knife back in my belt, and leaning over the edge reached through the hole in the canvas and found a handhold on the jagged edge of the blown-out wall.

For a long moment I hung there, my left hand on the ladder, my right hand on the radio room wall, trying to judge the motion of the ship. She rose up high on a wave crest, plunged heavily into a trough, and as she started back up, I swung my body to the right, pushed off from the ladder and rolled into the radio room, slamming against something hard and cutting my hands on some broken glass.

It was dark in the room, and the wind howling

through the hole in the canvas blew dust and grit everywhere.

I worked my way back to the opening and, bracing myself against the inside wall with one hand and one foot, looked outside.

Sharon was hanging on to the ladder less than three feet away, and when I reached my hand out to her, she cautiously let go of the ladder with her right hand and grabbed mine.

I was about to motion her to get ready to jump, when her feet slipped from the ladder and she fell sideways, twisting to the left, her entire weight suddenly pulling against my arm, nearly yanking it out of its socket and nearly pulling me through the opening.

For a long, terrible second, I was certain I would not be able to hold her, but then her body straightened out below, the ship came up again onto a wave crest, and I yanked with every ounce of my strength.

Sharon came up over the edge, teetered there for a moment, but then tumbled inside on top of me, both of us going down in a heap.

For a long time we were both content to lay there like that as we tried to catch our breath. No matter what else happened we would not try to go back the same way. We had been lucky enough climbing up here. I wasn't going to push our luck any further.

Finally we separated, and I pulled out the flashlight and flipped it on, the sight that greeted us momentarily taking my breath away.

The radio room was in a complete shambles, much worse than I thought it would be. I knew immediately that there would be absolutely nothing of any value to us here.

The explosion must have been tremendous. Besides tearing out the forward bulkhead and much of the roof, the force of the blast had bulged the starboard bulkhead, and had literally pulverized everything in the room.

On one side of the compartment was the shattered remains of a desk and what once had been some electronic equipment. Intermingled with the twisted steel, plastic, glass and copper wire, were vague reddish brown splotches.

Someone *had* been on duty up here when the explosion had been touched off, which proved that the Red Fist crewman had absolutely no regard for anyone's life.

There was no way we would be able to signal the Israeli gunboat from here. But at three o'clock A.M., when the ship approached the *Akai Maru*, the terrorist would undoubtedly blow the bombs. Somehow we had to stop him.

I got to my feet and went across the room to the shattered remains of the ship's communications equipment. The radio cabinets were bent and twisted, some of them smashed almost flat.

Sharon had gotten to her feet and joined me as I played the beam of the flashlight over the jumbled mess.

"It's no use," she said.

I looked at her. "Who is the second terrorist? Do you know his name? Have you seen him?"

She nodded. "Sal'Fit Quanrum. He and the other one signed on as ordinary seamen. I saw them both in Kuwait City."

"Their quarters would be aft on the main deck level, then," I said.

"What are you going to do?" she asked, her eyes wide.

"We have to find his bunk, grab the detonator and destroy it before he has a chance to blow the ship."

"That won't help stop the bombs I placed. The captain of the gunboat has got a detonator too."

"I know," I said. "But I don't think he'd sink this ship without getting the captain and crew off first."

"There's no way we could explain the presence of the gunboat out there," she said. "The plan was for me to tell the captain I was a terrorist and had planted bombs. He was supposed to radio for help. Our gunboat would be the nearest ship. Just by chance. This way, without a radio, we'd never be able to pull it off."

"We'll have to tell him the entire story," I said.

"No," she snapped, the expression on her face suddenly harsh and cold. She stepped back away from me, and before I could bring the Uzo around off my back, she had pulled out her gun and pointed it at me. "No one must know about the strontium 90."

"I do," I said softly. "And we either tell the captain or we run the risk that this ship will be sunk."

"I can't let it happen, Nick," she said. "You've got to understand that. If the Russians ever found out that Israel has nuclear capabilities, they would immediately equip Syria, Jordan, Lebanon and the others with nukes. We wouldn't have a chance."

I was about to tell her that this had been a Russian operation from the beginning, when the door from the companionway opened causing us to turn in surprise.

A short, thin man was framed in the doorway, the light from the corridor at his back, making it difficult for a moment to see his face.

He said something, jumped back and slammed the door before either Sharon or I could move.

"It's him!" she shouted. "Quanrum!"

ELEVEN

"The detonator," I shouted. I reached the door first, threw it open and leaped out into the companionway just as Quanrum was turning the corner a hundred feet away.

Sharon was right behind me and we headed in a dead run after the terrorist. If he made it to wherever he had hidden the detonator, everything would be lost.

The captain and one of his officers were just coming from the bridge, and when they spotted us coming down the companionway they both started to reach for their jacket pockets.

I flipped the Uzo around off my back, snapped the safety off and fired a quick burst over their heads. Both of them ducked down, fell back into the bridge and slammed the door behind them. A second later we had made it past the bridge hatch, had turned the corner and were pounding down the stairs.

Someone fired a shot from above as we reached the first landing down, the bullet ricocheting dangerously off the walls and stairs.

Sharon and I ducked around the corner into the companionway to get out of the line of fire.

"Stay back," I shouted up.

Four more shots were fired in quick succession, and I spun around the corner and fired a quick burst at the ceiling, the noise deafening in the narrow confines of the stairwell.

We were running out of time. The terrorist had too big a head start on us and we didn't know for sure where his quarters were, or even if he had hid the detonator there.

It was quiet above for several long seconds, and I turned to Sharon and nodded. Then both of us leaped back onto the landing and continued down, taking the stairs two and three at a time.

Just before we reached the main deck, there was a commotion of several men coming on the stairs above us, that was drowned out a moment later by the ship's fire alarm which began clanging throughout the vessel.

We burst out onto the main deck companionway at the same moment a half a dozen crewmen piled out of the mess. When they spotted us, they started to fall back.

I raised the machine gun and shouted, "Stop!"

The six of them froze in their tracks and raised their hands.

"Where is Quanrum's bunk?" I shouted in Japanese as Sharon and I moved quickly in their direction.

One of the crewmen looked toward the starboard side of the ship, and pointed that way to an open door. "There," he said, his voice shaky.

"Back inside," I ordered, motioning with the Uzo.

They practically fell all over each other scrambling back into the crew's mess, and Sharon and I raced down the companionway. At the open door we pulled up short.

I flattened myself against the bulkhead and eased around the corner. Quanrum, wearing a bulky life vest, was just straightening up from a locker beneath his bunk as I stepped around the corner, bringing the machine gun up.

He turned, a pistol in one hand and a small black box with a short antenna projecting from it in the other. He had a maniacal expression in his eyes.

"No closer!" he screamed, holding the black box over his head. His thumb was on the button.

My finger was on the trigger of the machine gun, but I eased back on the pressure. If I shot him now, reflex action would cause him to jerk his thumb on the detonator and the ship would blow.

"We'll let you go if you hand over the detonator," I said, trying to keep my voice even and to make myself heard over the noise of the fire alarm.

The compartment contained four bunks, two on each side of a narrow aisle. At the opposite end of the room was another doorway that evidently led to the aft companionway, which in turn led outside to the after deck.

Quanrum sidestepped out into the aisle and backed slowly toward the aft doorway.

"You don't want to die," I said, moving carefully into the room.

"No closer!" the man screamed. "I will blow up the ship!" He backed quickly to the doorway.

"Nick!" Sharon shouted, and she leaped into the room as someone out in the companionway opened fire.

"No!" Quanrum screamed. He pushed the button on the detonator and fired his gun, hitting me in my left leg well above my knee, spinning me around and knocking me to the deck.

Someone else fired at us from the companionway, and before I could regain my balance and bring the Uzo up into firing position, Quanrum had thrown down the detonator with a cry and had slipped out the aft door.

Evidently the bombs he had rigged below were on some kind of a delay fuse, giving him time to get off the ship.

I scrambled around behind the door and shoved it closed. A second later Sharon had thrown the latch and was helping me up.

The pain was coming at me in waves, making me dizzy, but apparently the bullet had only passed through the soft tissue in my leg and had not torn any muscles or broken any bones. I could still walk on it, and only a small amount of blood oozed from the wound.

"You're hurt," Sharon cried, and went to one of the bunks where she threw the blanket back and ripped a large piece of cloth from one of the sheets.

"I'm all right," I snapped. "He activated the detonator."

"He couldn't have," she said, looking up from what she was doing.

"The bombs must be on a delay fuse."

"No," she shouted, coming back to me with the cloth. "We both looked at them. There was no delay fuses there."

She took the knife from me, cut the leg of my jumpsuit and tied the cloth tightly around the wound. Already the shock of impact was beginning to wear off and the pain was becoming intense.

When she was finished, I hobbled between the

bunks to where Quanrum had thrown the detonator. If the bombs were not equipped with timers, then the delay mechanism had to be in the detonator unit itself.

I told Sharon as much when I had found the device and picked it off the floor. She took it from me.

"I've been trained in electronics," she said.

There was a commotion out in the aft companionway, and I brought the Uzo up and went to the doorway sticking the machine gun barrel around the corner.

Three crewmen were racing down the corridor our way.

"Back," I shouted, stepping out into the companionway.

They skidded to a halt. All of them were armed with rifles.

"Drop your weapons," I yelled over the noise of the fire alarm.

For several long seconds they just stood there staring at me.

"Drop your weapons!" I repeated in Japanese.

Slowly the three of them laid their rifles down on the deck and then carefully straightened up.

"Now get out of here and tell your captain the bombs will blow at any minute! Tell him to get ready to abandon ship!"

None of them moved.

"Go!" I shouted, raising the machine gun.

They spun around finally, raced down the companionway and out the portside hatch. I turned back to Sharon who had the back of the detonator unit off and was studying the mechanism.

"Can you take the batteries out or interrupt the timing circuit without setting the bombs off?" I asked.

She looked up at me, a confused expression in her eyes. "There is no timing mechanism here," she said.

"What?" I said. "There has to be."

"No," she said, and she handed the device to me. I studied the complicated circuitry inside, but could not see anything that even remotely looked like a timing device. The unit appeared to be nothing more than a subcompact transmitter of some kind, connected to a button that would send a signal.

"It's just a standard high-frequency signalling unit," Sharon said. "Could be used as a detonator, but there's definitely no timer there."

I looked at her. "Or it could be used as a signalling device? Nothing more?"

She nodded, obviously not understanding what I was getting at. But it had all become painfully clear to me. And if I was right, we were in bigger trouble than I had thought possible.

"We've got to get up to the bridge," I said.

"What?" Sharon asked confused. "I don't understand what you're talking about. What about the bombs? What about Quanrum?"

"The bombs were never meant to be detonated," I said. "At least not by Quanrum, with this." I held up the detonator.

"Then what, or by whom?"

"This is nothing more than a signalling device. If things got so bad aboard this ship for the terrorists that they felt they had to sink her, they would push the button. But instead of detonating the bombs like they thought the button would do, they only sent out a signal."

"To whom?" she practically shouted.

"To whoever else is out there shadowing us," I said. I knew full well who it was. But with Sharon's almost paranoid fear of what the Russians might do if they found out that the Israelis had nuclear capabilities, I didn't know how she might react if she was told this had been a Soviet plot from the beginning.

One thing definite I had learned from the dummy detonator, however, was that the Russians wanted the contaminated oil to reach the United States. The bombs had been placed aboard evidently as a last-ditch emergency measure. But the Russians definitely wanted the oil to reach the refineries at Bakersfield, California. Why?

I limped back out into the companionway that was still deserted. If there was a Russian vessel out there, the signal had already been sent and she would be closing in on the *Akai Maru* at this moment. Meanwhile the Israeli gunboat captain still held a detonator for the bombs Sharon had placed.

The only way out of this situation, as far as I could figure, would be to take over the ship and steer an evasive action course in order to alert the *Whiteshark* that I was in deep trouble.

Sharon followed me down the corridor to the portside hatch, which I undogged and opened. The storm had begun to die down and already the rain had stopped.

"Quanrum can still detonate at least one of the bombs," she said. "All he has to do is go down there and dislodge one of them. It'll blow."

I turned back. "I know," I said. "But he was wearing a life jacket. I'm betting he's already abandoned ship."

"Your people are out there, aren't they, Nick," she said.

I looked at her for a long minute, finally nodding my head.

"Plus whoever Quanrum was signaling."

I didn't say anything to that; instead I slipped out the hatch onto the main deck. The hatch to the forward companionway opened and I dropped down to my knee, a stab of pain coursing through me. I brought the machine gun up, but a moment later the hatch slammed shut with the motion of the ship.

"What is it?" Sharon shouted from behind me. At that same instant the ship's fire alarm stopped and we both looked back down the still deserted companionway we had just left.

The forward companionway hatch swung open again, clanging against the side of the ship, and closed once more as the vessel rolled with the next wave crest.

For a long moment I had the uncanny feeling that we were alone on the *Akai Maru,* that the ship had already been abandoned.

I got unsteadily to my feet and carefully moved forward to the hatch, peeking inside as the thick metal door swung open.

This companionway was deserted as well, and Sharon and I slipped inside, closing and latching the hatch behind us.

The only noise now was the thrumming of the engines far below us as the ship continued to plow through the waves. Even the wind had died down so that now we could no longer hear it moaning and howling around the superstructure.

"Where'd they go?" Sharon asked.

"I don't know," I said. Keeping close to the bulkhead, I moved down the companionway to the stairwell and looked inside. It too was deserted, the feeling growing inside me that perhaps the ship *had* been abandoned.

Sharon and I started up the stairs, moving as quickly as we could, but making absolutely no noise. At each deck we looked out into the companionway, but each time there was no one there. Nor was there any sound other than the engines.

I tried to think this out so I could determine what was happening here. The ship's fire alarm had been going and then was cut off. Perhaps the entire crew was on fire stations. But where would that be on an oil tanker?

I stepped out of the stairwell into the bridge deck companionway. The hatch to the bridge was open halfway down the companionway from where we stood. Beyond that, the radio room hatch was open as well, the wind from the motion of the ship howling through the doorway.

As we headed down the companionway I flipped the Uzo's safety off, and I noticed that Sharon did the same with her gun. I did not want to get into a position where I had to shoot one of the crewmen, yet I could not allow this ship to be sunk, by the Russians or by the Israelis.

We had gotten about halfway to the bridge hatch when someone came barreling up the stairwell and burst out into the companionway.

I swiveled around in time to see Sakai, a thick bandage wrapped around his head, charging at us.

Sharon raised her pistol and fired, hitting the man in the shoulder. But it didn't stop him, it didn't even slow him down.

Before she could fire another shot, the stocky Japanese batted her aside with a backhand, bouncing her off the bulkhead.

I jumped back and pointed the Uzo machine gun directly at his chest, the safety off, my finger on the trigger. I did not want to kill the man, but I felt that I was being forced into it.

He probably read the determination in my eyes because he pulled up short and crouched in the classic karate stance.

Sharon was dazed but she was starting to come around, her gun on the deck a couple of feet away from her.

I kept the machine gun leveled at Sakai's chest. "I don't want to hurt you or anyone else aboard this ship," I said in Japanese.

Sakai's expression did not change. It was as if he was waiting for me to put down my weapon and fight like a man on equal terms. Any other time I might have obliged him, although I had a strong suspicion of how the fight would come out. But now there was no time.

We were about ten feet apart and he took a step closer to me.

"Damnit!" I said. "I don't want to kill you, but if you force me into it, I will!"

Sharon had gotten to her knees and was rubbing her forehead. I backed up a step into the barrel of a gun at the base of my skull.

"Put your weapon down," the man behind me said. He must have come from the bridge.

Sakai started forward at the same moment

Sharon looked up, understood what was happening and lunged for her pistol laying on the deck.

Sakai heard the motion and he swiveled around as Sharon scooped up her pistol. She held it with both hands and pointed it up at the stocky Japanese's head. "Stop or I'll kill you!" she shouted.

Once again Sakai skidded to a halt, crouching in the karate stance.

"Tell your girlfriend to drop her weapon or I will shoot you," the man behind me said.

"Whatever you do this man will be dead," Sharon snapped. "And unless you're a better shot than I am, there's a very good chance I'll kill you as well."

"I'll shoot him," the man behind me said. I hadn't moved a muscle, but I could feel the sweat beading on my forehead.

"Shoot him and get it over with, or stand back and put your weapon down," Sharon said harshly. "Five seconds and I'm going to put a bullet between this man's eyes."

"No—" the man behind me started to shout, as I dropped to my knees, spun around and slammed the wire stock of the Uzo into his stomach. He went down.

"Don't!" Sharon shouted from behind me at Sakai who had started after her.

I scrambled over the top of the downed officer, grabbed the pistol from his hand, and with pain got to my feet behind him, the blood oozing from the cloth tied around the wound in my leg.

"On your feet," I said to the officer, who slowly got up, holding his stomach with both hands.

I glanced down toward the bridge hatch as I

stuffed the pistol in my pocket, then turned back to the officer. "Who else is on the bridge?"

The man looked at me, fear in his eyes.

I took a step toward him, raising the Uzo. "Who else is on the bridge?"

"The second officer and the helmsman," the man said.

"No one else?"

"No," the man said shaking his head.

"Where is the captain and the rest of the crew?" I snapped.

For a moment it seemed as if the officer was not going to answer me, but then he thought better of it. "There was a fire drill alarm," he said. "They're on the fire station below, on the main deck."

"The captain as well?"

"Yes."

I looked past the officer to where Sharon was still on her knees holding her gun in both hands, pointing it up at Sakai less than five feet from her.

"Are you all right?" I asked her.

"I'm all right, how about you?"

"Fine for the moment," I said, and I turned my attention back to the officer. That captain and crew were going to have to be warned about what I figured would be a certain attack by the Russians. If they were caught unaware, it would be slaughter. "I want you to listen very carefully now to what I'm going to tell you," I said. "We mean you or this ship no harm, you must believe that. But you are going to come under an armed attack very soon and there is a possibility that this ship may be sunk. Tell your captain to get his crew out of sight. Arm them if you have the weapons, but keep them out of sight and ready to abandon ship."

"Who are you and why are you doing this to us?" the officer asked.

"That doesn't matter," I snapped. "What does matter is for you to get that message to your captain."

The officer stared at me, hatred in his eyes. "You will never get off of this ship alive."

"None of us will unless you do as I say," I said. "Now get out of here, and take Sakai with you. We're running out of time and I don't want to hurt either of you."

The officer looked at me for a very long time, as if he was memorizing my face, then he turned and said something to Sakai in rapid-fire Japanese.

At first Sakai didn't move. The officer shouted at him again and the stocky Japanese straightened up, looked over his shoulder at me, then he and the other man went past Sharon, turned the corner and started down the stairs.

Sharon got to her feet and hurried after me as I turned and limped the rest of the way down the companionway to the open bridge hatch, and slipped inside.

The bridge was contained in a huge room that ran nearly the entire width of the ship. It was lit only by the soft red glow of several lights set flush in the ceiling and by the light coming from hundreds of dials and gauges on the equipment.

A young man in a white uniform stood behind a huge stainless steel wheel at the center of the bridge; to his left, speaking on a telephone while staring out the windows, was the second officer.

"Watch the companionway," I said softly to Sharon, and I went all the way into the huge room.

The deck officer saw my reflection in the window

as I crossed the room, and he spun around, his mouth agape.

"Put the telephone down," I said in Japanese.

The young helmsman nearly jumped out of his skin and he turned around to stare at me.

"Put it down," I snapped, raising the machine gun.

The deck officer put the telephone down and raised his hands over his head. "What do you want?" he asked.

"Lock the helm on course," I said to the young man, but he didn't move a muscle.

"Tell him!" I shouted at the deck officer.

"There's someone coming," Sharon shouted from the doorway.

"Hold them off," I called back, and I motioned with the Uzo. "Tell him to lock the helm on course."

"Do as he says," the deck officer said. The helmsman looked from me to his officer, and then pulled a large stainless-steel lever on the steering pedestal down and stepped away from the wheel, his hands raised over his head.

"Tell them we're sending two of their people out," I shouted over my shoulder at Sharon.

I could hear her relaying my instructions to whoever was out in the companionway.

"You can't run this ship by yourselves," the deck officer said.

I stepped to one side and motioned with the machine gun toward the hatch. "Get out of here. Both of you."

"You can't do this—"

"Goddamnit, I said get out of here! Now!"

The man jumped, and he and the helmsman sidestepped past me, hurried across to the doorway and carefully eased past Sharon, who had flattened herself against the bulkhead.

When they had cleared the doorway she stepped back, slammed the hatch closed, dogged it and slid the locking lever in place.

She joined me a moment later by the helm and we both let out a long sigh of relief. We were in control of the ship, at least for the moment.

"What now?" she asked.

I pulled out a cigarette, lit it and inhaled deeply. "We change course to the starboard for three minutes, to the port for three minutes and back to the starboard for three minutes."

"S.O.S.," she said, and I nodded. "Who's out there?"

"One of our submarines."

"No, I mean who did Quanrum signal? Who will be attacking this ship?"

"A Russian destroyer, I imagine," I said. "Or perhaps a submarine."

Her complexion turned a pasty color. "The Soviets. . ." she started to say, but the words died in her throat.

"This was a Soviet plot all along, Sharon," I said, and I quickly recounted for her what I had found in Kuwait City as well as in Beirut.

"You're sure they were KGB agents?" she asked.

I nodded. "They definitely were Russian and they carried Soviet embassy ID cards. They were KGB all right."

"My God," she said softly. "Everything is lost now."

"Not yet," I said. I released the locking mecha-

nism that held the helm on course and spun the
huge wheel to the right all the way to its stops, and
the huge ship began to respond sluggishly as she
turned off the wind and began smashing into the
waves at an ever increasing angle.

TWELVE

Sharon found a well-stocked first aid kit in one of the storage cabinets on the back bulkhead of the bridge by the time I started the second series of right-left-right maneuvers.

With shaky hands she set the case down at my feet, opened it, and with a pair of scissors cut the cloth from around the wound. Next she cut the blood-soaked trouser leg off and threw it aside.

"Does it hurt much?" she asked looking up at me.

"Can't feel a thing," I lied, concentrating on what I was doing.

The weather had calmed down considerably, but the wind was still stiff and the seas were running fifteen to twenty feet, occasionally spraying over the bow when the *Akai Maru* bit deeply into a trough.

So far we had seen no sign of the Israelis or the Russians, but I was sure that the *Whiteshark* was by now aware that something was definitely wrong here by the erratic movements of the ship.

"This is going to sting," Sharon said, and I was about to look away from the compass to tell her to go ahead with whatever she was going to do, when

172

a tremendous stab of pain hit me. For an instant it seemed as if she had cut my leg off with a rusty axe. The agony was so bad that it brought spots in front of my eyes.

Someone was calling my name then, from the end of a very long tunnel. My stomach was flopping over, and the room seemed very hot. I could feel the sweat pouring from me.

"Nick . . . Nick?" Sharon called my name again, and I opened my eyes surprised to see her above me.

"What—" I tried to say, but it only came out as a mumble, and I realized that I was lying on the deck, the pain in my leg receding into a dull throb. My stomach was beginning to settle down, too.

"Are you all right?" she was saying. "You fainted."

I tried to sit up, but could not seem to manage until Sharon helped me. "What the hell happened?" I asked, finally getting a hold of myself.

"I poured some alcohol on your wound and you went out like a light."

I looked up into her concerned eyes and managed a weak smile. I still felt queasy. "Warn me after this if you're going to do anything like that."

"I told you it would sting," she said.

I had to laugh, the sound ragged. "That's an understatement," I croaked. "I thought you had cut my leg off."

"You've lost a lot of blood," she told me. "I think we should get the doctor up here."

She had bandaged my leg with thick gauze pads, but already a spot of blood the size of a half dollar had soaked through.

"How long was I down?" I asked, struggling up

on my good knee with her help.

"About five minutes, maybe a little longer," she said, and with her help I made it to my feet, resting most of my weight on my good leg.

For several long moments I had to hold on to Sharon with one hand and the wheel with the other to keep from falling flat on my face. Finally the room stopped spinning and I was able to stand on my own.

I turned toward the windows and scanned the dark horizon in every direction, but I could not see a thing. It meant nothing, however. A ship running without lights would be almost totally invisible until it came right on top of us.

As I turned back to Sharon I was sure I could smell smoke. She evidently had smelled it as well, because she wrinkled up her nose.

"Fire?" she said looking up at me, and we both turned toward the bridge hatch where a thin curl of smoke was coming from around a cherry red line that slowly moved around the lower hinge.

It took me just a split second to realize what was happening. The crew had obviously brought a cutting torch up here and they were burning the hinges off the hatch. By the looks of their progress, it would only be a matter of minutes before they would have the hatch down.

Once they rushed us it would be over, because there was no way I could bring myself to shoot innocent men who were doing nothing more than protecting their own ship from saboteurs and hijackers.

"Find a pry bar or a metal rod, something I can jam the steering mechanism with," I snapped.

Sharon raced across the room to the line of supply cabinets against the aft bulkhead as I spun the wheel all the way to the left. If we could find something to lock the steering in that position, the ship would continue to make huge circles until the trouble was fixed, further alerting the *Whiteshark* that something had gone wrong.

The bottom hinge of the hatch broke loose and by the time Sharon had returned with a fire axe, the red line was already working its way around the upper hinge.

For several seconds I studied the steering mechanism and pedestal for its most vulnerable point, and finally I saw how it could be done.

With the wheel all the way over to the left and the ship starting to turn to port, I engaged the wheel locking lever.

"Get back," I said to Sharon, and as she stepped back I moved into position in front of the steering pedestal and swung the heavy axe with all my might, hitting the steering lock lever at its swivel point. The axe clanged against the metal, bending the lever nearly half off. On the second hit, the lever snapped off just as the top hinge of the hatch broke loose.

I put the axe down, took the pistol from my pocket and laid it in plain sight on the deck, motioning for Sharon to do the same with her gun. The Uzo was laying over on the chart table.

Then both of us stepped back from the helm and stood by the windows as the hatch fell inward with a crash, and a half a dozen armed crewmen rushed onto the bridge.

For several confused seconds I was sure the over-agitated men would shoot us, but then the captain strode through the doorway, his jacket open, his hair mussed, a wild look in his eyes, and he shouted for silence.

Instantly his crewmen froze in their positions, the only sound now the thrumming of the distant engines.

The captain came across the bridge to us, and without warning smashed his fist into my jaw. My head snapped back, bouncing off the window frame behind me and I staggered to my knees. Sharon reached down to try and help me, but the captain backhanded her halfway across the room.

I started to get to my feet when the captain turned back to me, grabbed me by the front of my jumpsuit, pulled me up and kicked me in my wounded leg.

The room was instantly hot, sounds were jumbled in a high-pitched whine and my vision blurred. He kicked me in my bad leg again and suddenly the only thing I was even vaguely aware of was my heart beating nearly out of my chest.

". . . answers . . ." I heard the disconnected word, and from a distance I heard what sounded like a woman screaming.

I struggled to hold on and gradually the room started to come back into focus.

"We're going to talk and I want the answers," the captain was shouting at me. He was holding me up against the window, his face inches from mine.

"If I have to kill you and your girlfriend I will, but first I want the answers!" the man screamed. He was insane. I was almost certain of it. The doctor had called the captain a man of extraordinary temper, but it was more than that.

He shook me, my head bouncing several times off the window frame, causing a deep, dark anger to well up inside of me. I understood the man's provocation, but he had gone too far.

I dropped down slightly, then brought both fists up under his arms, knocking his hands loose from my shoulders. In the next instant, before the captain or anyone else could react, I pushed away from the wall, slamming my shoulder into the man's chest, knocking him flat on his back. Then I leaped on top of him, my left forearm behind his neck and the palm of my right hand under his chin. I lifted him half off the deck and pushed his head way back so he could hardly breathe.

"Anyone moves and I break your captain's neck," I shouted.

The man tried to fight me, so I pushed his head back a little further.

"Put down your weapons!" I shouted. The captain's face was starting to turn blue, and his struggles were getting weaker. "Your captain will die very soon unless you do as I say. Immediately!"

"Do it," someone else said.

I looked up as the doctor came across the room. He was carrying his medical bag. Our eyes met for a moment.

"Put your weapons down, you fools, he means what he says," the doctor shouted.

One by one the crewmen laid their weapons on the deck.

"Sharon?" I called out. I couldn't see her.

"Here, Nick," she said from behind me.

I looked over my shoulder to where she stood by the windows, a large red welt forming on her cheek and a small trickle of blood coming from her mouth. "Get the Uzo," I said. "On the chart table."

She hurried across the bridge, grabbed the machine gun from where I had laid it and snapped the safety off.

I let go of the captain, and very painfully got to my feet and stepped back.

The doctor rushed forward and dropped down next to the captain who was dazed, but already coming around.

I hung onto the steering wheel for support, my vision coming in and out of focus.

The doctor helped the captain to sit up, and then a minute later get to his feet. For a moment the man stood there glaring at me and then he tried to totter forward, but the doctor stopped him.

"I couldn't let the man beat me to death," I said tiredly.

"Can you blame him?" the doctor snapped harshly. "What do you want with this ship? Why are you trying to kill us?"

"We aren't," I said. "Two of your crewmen are Soviet agents. They blew up your radio room and killed your radio operator."

"I don't believe you—" the doctor started to say, but the captain broke in.

"The two we signed on at Al Kuwait?" he asked, his voice hoarse.

I nodded. "Quanrum was one of them."

"The other was Ahmid al Fais'el," Sharon said from where she stood holding the machine gun.

"Fais'el is missing," the captain said looking over at her.

Sharon nodded. "I killed him."

"Quanrum sent a signal to a Soviet vessel out there somewhere," I said, "and then he probably abandoned ship. He's got the entire vessel rigged with plastique explosives."

"No," one of the officers at the back spoke up. "Unless he jumped overboard."

Everyone turned toward him. "The lifeboats are all intact?" the captain snapped.

"Aye aye, sir," the officer said. "If Quanrum abandoned ship, he didn't take a boat and he's certainly dead by now."

The captain turned back to me. "What interest do the Soviets have with this vessel?" he asked.

Quanrum was surely a fanatic, but I did not think the man was a complete fool. If none of the lifeboats was missing, I could not imagine him jumping overboard into twenty-foot seas. It did not make sense. The only other alternative then was for him to still be aboard and most likely below deck where he might set off one of the bombs.

And on top of all that, the Israeli gunboat was still out there. The captain had a detonator for Sharon's bombs.

"It's all lies," the captain said.

"No," I shouted.

"Then answer my question. What possible interest could the Soviet government have in a shipload of crude oil?"

"Nick?" Sharon said, and I turned toward her.

"We can't," she shouted, raising the machine gun slightly. The crew members stepped back.

"Their lives are at stake here, Sharon," I argued. "We have to tell them. The politicians can work it out later."

She was having a hard time dealing with what I was saying to her.

"Put the gun down," I said softly.

She looked at me, her eyes wide. "After what they've done to us?"

"Put the gun down," I repeated. "Quanrum is still aboard. He's probably below deck now getting ready to set off one of his bombs. And I don't think it will take the Russians very long to attack. We're running out of time."

I was sweating, the room hot again, and my stomach was churning. The wound in my leg throbbed all the way up my side and into my shoulder.

A deathly silence fell over the bridge, and finally Sharon slowly turned around and laid the machine gun on the chart table, then turned back to us.

The captain started toward me, but again the doctor held him back.

"Guns or no guns, captain," I said, a very harsh edge to my voice. "You raise a hand against me again and I will beat you to death. And that is a promise."

No one had made a move for their weapons, but I knew that one word, one gesture from the captain, and we would be cut down.

"You said we were running out of time," the doctor spoke up.

I nodded. "Whether you believe this or not, is totally up to you, but it is the truth."

"We're listening," the doctor said.

"A Lebanese terrorist group, calling themselves the Red Fist of November managed to steal a canister of strontium 90. It's a very deadly radio-active material."

"I know what it is," the doctor said.

"Where did they get it?" the captain said, a surly edge to his voice.

I glanced over at Sharon whose face was white. She was holding herself rigid. "That doesn't matter," I said, turning back. "But I know for a fact that the group got the material and were helped by the Russians."

"What does that have to do with us?" the captain snapped.

"The material was taken out of its container and brought aboard this ship."

"Impossible," the doctor protested.

I shook my head. "No. Four of the people who handled the stuff died of extreme radioactive poisoning. I don't know exactly how Quanrum and Fais'el got the stuff aboard this ship, probably in some other kind of a container, but they did."

"Where is it?" the captain asked.

I took a deep breath and let it out slowly. "They dumped it in the oil."

"What . . ." the captain barely breathed the single word.

"They dumped it in the oil. Your entire five million gallons of crude is slightly radioactive."

"Why? Why do something like that?"

"I don't know. It was one of the reasons I was sent out here."

"By whom?" the doctor asked.

I looked at him. "I can't tell you that."

"You're an American. CIA?"

I shook my head. "I don't work for the CIA. I've told you the truth so far, and I'm telling you the truth in this. But that's all you need to know."

"What about the Russian ship you say is out there getting ready to attack us?" the doctor asked.

"I'm only guessing about it. But when we cornered Quanrum in his quarters, he had what I took to be a detonating device for the bombs he had placed below deck. He pressed the button before we could stop him, but nothing happened. When we examined the device it turned out to be nothing more than a signalling transmitter, signalling presumably a Soviet vessel standing by in case there was trouble."

"That doesn't make any sense," the doctor said. "If, as you've told us, the Russians did manage to contaminate the oil aboard this ship, why would they attack us now?"

"I don't know that either," I had to admit. "I don't even know why they contaminated the oil in the first place. I don't think it was ever their intention to sink this ship, therefore spilling the radioactive oil."

"Which means they want the oil to get to the refineries at Bakersfield," the captain said. "Is that what you're trying to tell us?"

Suddenly it struck me. The entire incredible thing suddenly made a terrible kind of sense. It was awesome. The sudden understanding must have shown on my face.

"You just figured it out," the doctor said.

I looked at him. "I'm afraid I have," I said.

"What is it, Nick?" Sharon asked. "What is it they're trying to do?"

"The oil is radioactive," I said slowly. "But not so radioactive that it will kill anyone who comes into contact with it. At least not immediately."

"Leukemia," the doctor said in a hushed tone. "And a dozen other kinds of carcinomas."

"That's right," I said. "The oil will be off-loaded in Bakersfield, and then will be refined into gasoline for the most part, gasoline that will be burned by automobiles all up and down our West coast.''

"The exhaust fumes would be slightly radio-active as well,'' the doctor said. "It would take years, perhaps as long as twenty, but then there would be a very dramatic rise in deaths due to cancer. Birth defects. Hundreds of symptoms. And by then it would be far too late to trace it back.''

For a very long time no one said a word. All of us were awed by the immensity of what was happening.

Finally the captain spoke. "If the Russians want the oil to get to Bakersfield, why did they rig this ship with explosives? And why do you think they will attack us now?''

"The explosives, I think, were nothing more than a concession to the terrorists who brought the strontium 90 aboard—'' I started to say, but then I stopped.

"What is it?'' Sharon asked.

"That's not it at all,'' I said, the rest of the in-sanely brilliant plan coming clear in my mind. "In theory the strontium 90 was supposed to be dumped in the oil, contaminating it. They managed that all right. Next Fais'el and Quanrum were sup-posed to rig the ship with explosives so that when she blew she'd sink immediately to the bottom. They managed that, too.''

"But the detonator Quanrum had wasn't real,'' Sharon objected.

"Of course not,'' I said. "If we hadn't in-terfered, this ship would have docked at Bak-ersfield, the oil would have been off-loaded, and on her return trip—empty—the Russians would have detonated the bombs. The ship would have sunk to the bottom, all hands lost. Absolutely no trace of what had happened would have ever been found."

"Quanrum carried what he thought was a detonator, to use if something happened," Sharon said.

"That's right," I agreed. "If somehow their plan was exposed, Quanrum was instructed to push the button. But instead of detonating the bombs, it signalled the Russian ship out there somewhere, that something had happened. They'd come aboard, take over the ship and deliver the oil themselves. Later, on the way back, they'd sink her, obliterating all traces of what they had done." I turned back to the captain. "What's the procedure in Bakersfield? Do you know anyone there personally?"

The captain shook his head, obviously not at all impressed by what we had told him. "We don't go through customs or passport control or anything," he said. "The oil is pumped out of the holds at the offshore station."

"That's it then," I said.

The captain stuck his hands in his jacket pockets and shook his head. "Do you expect me to believe all that?"

I knew damned well he had a gun in his pocket, but there wasn't a thing I could do about it. The Uzo was behind Sharon, and the pistol I had taken from the man out in the companionway was lying on the deck a few feet to my left.

Our only hope now was the *Whiteshark*. But she had not surfaced yet, and if the Russians didn't take us or the Israelis didn't push the detonator button, Quanrum would probably set off one of the bombs in the hold. Whatever things did not look very good at the moment.

"Take the gun out of your pocket, captain, and

show us just what kind of a man you are," I said. "When the Russians do attack you'll be able to change your mind about everything."

The captain's eyes blazed as he pulled the .38 Police Special out of his pocket, cocked the hammer and pointed it at me.

"I know what the captain is going to say and I share his views," the doctor said.

I turned to the man and smiled. "We're here to hijack the ship and her oil."

The doctor inclined his head. "It would bring a tidy sum."

"If we could sell it," I said. "And if you think the story I told you about the strontium 90 was good, wait until you hear about our plans for disguising this ship as a three-hundred foot commercial fishing vessel."

"Captain!" one of the crewmen shouted in abject terror.

Everyone turned toward the man whose eyes were wide. He was pointing toward the windows.

I spun around in time to see five or six assault helicopters hovering twenty feet over the decks, disgorging dozens of troops. A large red star was painted on the fuselage of every olive-drab machine.

THIRTEEN

"If you believe those are my people then you're a bigger fool than I gave you credit for," I shouted at the captain.

The man had leaped to the windows and was watching the Soviet troops storming his ship. The rest of his crew were frozen in position, not knowing what to do.

"Bust out all the windows," I snapped as I scooped up my pistol and the one Sharon had laid on the floor.

"We can't fight them," the doctor shouted. "It would be suicide!"

"Listen, Doc," I said coming back to him. "The Russians are here to take over this ship! They'll kill every one of you! When they have control of her, they're going on to Bakersfield to deliver the oil! They won't be able to do it if the ship is busted up!"

Sharon grabbed the Uzo machine gun from the chart table and joined us.

"Break out every window on the bridge and then have your people start shooting." I looked around the room. The captain was still staring out the window, the gun in his hand hanging limply at his side.

"Bust up all the gear in this room that you can as well," I said. "The more damage you can inflict the harder it will be for them to complete their mission."

"What about you?" the doctor said.

"Sharon and I are going to try to make the engine room. If we can sabotage the engines they'll never get her into Bakersfield."

"No," the captain shouted. Sharon and I spun around toward him. He was pointing the gun at us. "You will not destroy this ship!" he screamed. "I will not allow it!"

"Those are Soviet shock troops out there, captain," I shouted. "They mean to kill you and your entire crew."

"I won't allow it—" the captain started to shout, when a six point metal star buried itself in his chest. He staggered back under the impact and tried to raise the pistol, but crumpled to the deck without a sound.

Sakai strode through the hatchway, his shoulder bandaged. I started to raise my pistol but he shook his head.

"I'm here to help you," he said in English, his voice obviously cultured.

"Do you know what's happening?" I asked.

"Everyone knows what's going on," he said. "The ship's intercom was left on. Everything that has been said here on the bridge has been piped throughout the ship."

"You're in charge, doc," I said. "Bust up the bridge as best you can."

Sakai came across the room and knelt down beside his captain. "Poor bastard," he said softly.

The doctor was obviously frightened and deeply

shocked by the murder of the captain, but he was a good man and I knew he would do his best.

A moment later Sharon and I joined Sakai back out in the companionway, and the three of us raced to the stairwell and started down. We could hear the sounds of fighting below.

"I stationed a half a dozen men in the main companionway to defend the port and starboard hatches," Sakai said as we pounded down the stairs.

The main entrance to the engine room stairwell was from the aft companionway, but we had to pass across the main corridor in order to get to it. Unless Sakai's men could keep the area clear, we would not be able to reach the engine room.

"Is there another way down to the engines from here?" I shouted as we continued down.

"There's an access tunnel from the aft deck, plus the bilge pumping wells on the forward decks," Sakai shouted over his shoulder.

The forward decks were out, that's where the Soviet troops were landing, which left the stairwell off the aft companionway or the aft deck if we could reach it.

We made it to the second deck landing, the fighting below now very intense. I motioned for Sakai and Sharon to hold back, and I eased around the corner in time to see one of the seamen below fall under heavy fire. A couple of seconds later a Soviet trooper rounded the corner and I shot him twice in the chest, then ducked back around the corner.

"They've gotten past your people already," I said. I gave Sharon the pistol and took the Uzo from her, snapping in a full clip. I swung around the corner in time to see two Soviets heading toward me in a dead run.

I sprayed the stairwell and both of them tumbled backward on top of the first man lying in a heap near the downed seaman.

Again I ducked back. "There's no way we're going to make it across the main companionway," I said. "Is there another way down?"

"I don't think so—" Sakai started to say, but he stopped in mid-sentence. "Wait. There is one possibility."

A tear gas canister clattered up from below, and immediately we were enveloped in a thick, choking mist. We all fell back away from the stairwell.

"This way," Sakai said, and he turned and raced down the companionway.

About a hundred feet down the corridor, Sakai opened a hatch in the aft bulkhead and ducked inside, Sharon and I directly on his heels.

I slammed the hatch closed after us and dogged the latches.

We were in a very large room that was filled with bins of fresh fruit and vegetables, cases of canned goods and a row of freezers and refrigerators.

"This is one of the crew's mess supply rooms," Sakai said from the opposite side of the room. He had gotten down on his hands and knees next to what appeared to be air conditioning vents of some kind that came up from the deck below.

Sharon and I joined him as he was unsnapping a large access plate from the side of one of the ducts.

Inside was a large electrical motor. Sakai stuck his head into the opening, seemed to be studying something a moment and then withdrew.

"This leads to the galley, directly above the cook stove," he said. "The grease filter is just a couple of feet below the motor."

He moved aside so that I could take a look. The duct was at least three feet on a side. A few feet below the large electrical motor and fan blades, I could see the upper section of the filter that was directly above the stove. There was no way we could get past the motor and fan, however. They would have to be removed.

I pulled out the duct. "We'll need some tools to get the motor out of there," I said, but Sakai smiled, and gently pushed me aside.

"What are you going to do?" I asked, but he said nothing as he got into a squat, reached inside the ductwork and fumbled around until he got a good grip on the motor.

Suddenly I realized what he was going to try. But it was impossible. No man could rip a two hundred pound motor from its mountings.

I was about to tell him that, when the muscles in his arm and neck suddenly bulged, his face turned red, his shirt ripped out at the shoulders and across the back, and with a rending of metal, the motor came free of its mountings. Sakai fell back, rolling the heavy motor over on the deck.

"My God," Sharon breathed the words, and I realized once and for all that no matter what happened, I would never attempt any kind of hand-to-hand combat with this monster of a man.

"Are you all right?" I asked as I helped him sit up.

He looked up at me and smiled. "Nothing to it," he said breathlessly as he tried to catch his wind. "All a matter of leverage."

Something slammed at the hatch, shaking the entire bulkhead.

"What was that?" Sharon shouted.

"I don't know," I said. "But if they keep it up, they'll be in here in a couple of minutes."

Something slammed at the hatch again, sounding like some kind of a battering ram. The Russians had come prepared.

Inside the ducting the fan blades were hanging loosely by a thin strip of metal, and holding onto the framework that the motor had been attached to, I stuck my legs through the opening, kicked the blades away and lowered myself down.

I hung there for several seconds trying to listen for any sounds from the galley below, but then the battering ram the Soviets were using clanged against the hatch and I kicked downward, knocking the filter out of its slots.

I dropped down on top of the ten burner cookstove as I swung the Uzo around. But the galley was deserted, both the forward and aft hatches closed.

"Come on," I shouted up as the jackhammer slammed against the hatch again.

Sharon came first, and I helped her down to the top of the stove and then down to the deck. A moment later Sakai's bulk filled the ducting, and he started to ease himself down as the jackhammer slammed against the hatch again.

"They're through!" he said, dropping down to the stove.

We jumped down to the deck and raced to the aft hatch, which Sharon undogged and opened a crack. A moment later she yanked it all the way open.

"It's clear," she said, and she slipped out into a long, narrow room filled with shelves of pots and pans on one side, and foodstuffs on the other.

At the opposite end of the storage room was another hatch.

"That opens directly on the aft deck," Sakai said. "Cookie goes out this way to throw the slops over the rail."

There was a small porthole in the hatch and Sharon looked outside. "It's clear," she said, and she undogged the hatch and eased it open.

We could hear the sounds of intense fighting forward, but it could not last much longer. The crewmen were evidently putting up a good fight, but they were certainly no match for the Soviet shock troops.

The clouds were starting to break up and several patches of stars were visible above the still choppy sea. Aft, the *Akai Maru* was leaving a wide, luminescent wake that stretched behind us for as far as I could see.

Somewhere out there was the Israeli gunboat with the detonator for Sharon's bombs, as well as the *Whiteshark*. One could sink us, the other could save us. Neither was in sight.

Sakai had pulled up a thick metal plate set flush in the deck, and Sharon and I started down the access tunnel. A few moments later Sakai had climbed down after us, closing the hatch, plunging us once again into total darkness.

The thumping sounds of the engines was much louder here, and the farther down we climbed the louder it became.

About thirty feet down I looked up as something dripped down on my sleeve. It was blood, I was sure of it.

"Sakai?" I called up. "Are you all right?"

He mumbled something in Japanese, but it was too indistinct for me to catch.

"What's wrong, Nick?" Sharon called to me from below.

"It's Sakai," I said. "I think he's hurt." I pulled the flashlight from my pocket, switched it on and pointed it upward.

Sakai was ten feet above me hunched up against the ladder, blood dripping from the wound in his shoulder which he must have pulled open when he yanked the motor from the galley exhaust duct.

"Sakai?" I shouted, but the man did not move.

"He's hurt badly," I shouted down to Sharon, and I started up to him.

"Go," he shouted, the word sounding slurred, almost as if he was drunk. "Engine room . . . go . . ." he said again, this time his voice much weaker.

I reached him a few moments later and scrambled up the side of the ladder so that I was level with his shoulder.

"You can't stay here," I said gently. "We've got to try to get you below so we can bandage your wound."

"Go," he said looking over at me. "Can't let them take the ship."

He started to lose his grip, but I held him in place with one hand, while maintaining a precarious hold with the other.

"Hang on Sakai," I said. "Just a little while longer. You've got to help me get you below."

He mumbled something else, but I couldn't catch it. Blood was pouring out of the wound in his shoulder, and the only explanation I could think of was that he had torn something in his chest when he strained to pull the motor out of the ductwork.

I let go of his shoulder and started to reach around him to grab the other side of the ladder when his body went loose and he slipped away.

"Look out Sharon!" I shouted dropping the flashlight.

She screamed. I could hear Sakai's body banging against the rungs of the ladder and the walls of the tunnel, and seconds later there was a muffled thump that caused me to wince involuntarily. My flashlight hit the bottom an instant later and went out. Then there was a silence in the tunnel except for the thrumming of the engines.

A half a second later I would have had a firm grip on him, I told myself. A half a second.

"Nick?" Sharon's voice came up to me.

"Are you all right?" I said, and I started down.

"I can't go any farther," she whimpered.

"Hang on Sharon," I said. I reached her a few moments later, climbing down the side of the ladder and cradling her body with mine. She was shivering.

"It was blood," she said. "He was bleeding."

"You've got to pull yourself together," I said. "The submarine that brought me here is coming. It'll be all right. You've just got to hang on a little longer."

"I can't, Nick," she cried. "Oh God, I can't do it any longer!"

"You must!" I shouted. "I can't do it alone, Sharon. I need your help."

"Nick?" she sobbed, and her body went slack.

I held on as tightly as I could, holding her with my own body as she cried herself out. The both of us had spent what seemed like a hundred years, being cold, wet and in pain. My head throbbed, the wound in my leg was bleeding again making my entire side numb, I was cold, tired, hungry and concerned about the *Whiteshark*. If Farmington had seen the erratic movements I had put the *Akai Maru* through, he surely would have been here by now. Which meant either he had not seen or understood what I was doing, or he wasn't out there after all.

I've always been very independent, I was trained to be. But at that moment I felt as if I had finally run into odds that were just too great to handle.

"I'm sorry, Nick," Sharon whimpered at long last. "I shouldn't be this way, but I'm frightened."

"So am I," I said softly, and I kissed her.

For a long while we clung together on the ladder as the fighting raged overhead. We were on our own. The crew had surely fallen by now, or soon would, and there was nothing left for us except to somehow sabotage the ship's engines so that the Russians would not be able to bring the ship to the Bakersfield off-loading island.

"Are you ready?" I asked.

"Yes," Sharon answered, and I eased down past her and continued into the bowels of the ship.

The ladder continued down another twenty-five feet, ending on a wide platform. When I stepped off, my left foot bumped into something soft. It was Sakai's body.

Sharon joined me a moment later.

"Have you got a flashlight?" I asked.

"Yes," she said, and she pulled it from her pocket and switched it on.

Sakai moaned and tried to sit up. He was still alive! I dropped down beside him.

"Don't try to talk," I said. Blood completely covered the front of his white uniform, and as he tried to speak again something gurgled in the back of his throat and blood oozed from his mouth.

"Companionway. . ." he wheezed. "Engine room companionway below."

There wasn't a thing we could do for him here. And I suspected that even under normal circumstances, if we could have gotten him to the dispensary, there would have been nothing the doctor could have done for him either. He was broken up inside. It was amazing he had lasted this long.

"They'll be in the engine room," he said with great difficulty.

"Don't talk—" I started to say, but he grabbed my arm and squeezed it. There was an intensity in his eyes.

"Get me down there . . . I can help . . ."

"We can't move you," I said. Sharon was staring down at him, a horrified expression on her face.

"I don't want to die here in this hole," Sakai said. "Don't let me die here. Let me help."

Again a deep, overwhelming anger built up inside of me. I wanted to lash out, I wanted to leap into the engine room companionway and kill anything or anyone who got in my way. One name kept hammering through my brain. *Kobelev*. If I somehow survived this, I was going after the insane creature. Wherever he was, whatever it took, I was going after the man who had planned this operation.

Even in failure Kobelev was responsible for dozens of deaths. Paul Bridley and his son back in Kuwait City were the most useless, the hardest to accept.

"We'll get you down there," I said, and Sakai

managed a crooked smile. "We'll get you there," I repeated.

I took the flashlight from Sharon and we hurried along the low, narrow catwalk until I found a hatch in the deck which I undogged and opened just a crack. Ten or twelve feet below was the engine room companionway, the stairwell to the right, the doorway down to the engine room itself about thirty feet to the left.

Two Russians and several of the *Akai Maru*'s crew were lying dead near the stairwell, and from above, over the sounds of the engines, I could hear sporadic gunfire.

I opened the hatch all the way. "Stay here, I'll get Sakai," I said to Sharon and she nodded, but said nothing.

I hurried back along the catwalk to where Sakai was laying on his side now, in a pool of blood. His eyes were open but he was not breathing.

For a long time I knelt down beside him, the fingertips of my right hand feeling for a pulse at his neck. But there was none. He was dead.

"Goddamnit," I breathed the single word as I looked down at him. The anger welled up inside of me again and it took several seconds for me to regain control of myself.

Finally I turned him over on his back and gently closed his eyes, then turned and hurried back to where Sharon was watching the companionway from the open hatch.

"Sakai?" she asked.

"He's dead."

She turned to look back down into the companionway. "The fighting has stopped," she whispered.

We both held our breath listening for any sounds

other than the engines. But there was nothing. The Russians had taken over the ship, which meant the crew was all dead.

I had switched the flashlight off and stuffed it in my pocket, then eased my body through the hatch and dropped down as quietly as I could into the companionway below. Instantly I pulled the Uzo around off my back and snapped the safety off.

The ship was quiet, and a few seconds later I looked up at Sharon and motioned for her to come down.

She came through the opening feet first. I reached up and helped her down. She took her gun from her pocket, flipped the safety off and together we hurried down the companionway where we pulled up just before the engine room doorway.

I got down on my stomach, eased to the edge of the opening and looked inside. There were four So-viet troops below near the main control board. Three of them were studying the various dials and controls, while the other one was speaking into a walkie-talkie. They all had their backs to us. All of them were armed with Koshelnikov assault rifles.

I wriggled back out of sight and sat up. "There's four of them down there," I said softly. There was no way we could be a hundred percent sure of tak-ing all of them out from here.

I glanced over toward the stairwell. Every sec-ond that we remained here in the companionway we ran the risk of someone coming down from topside. If that happened, we would be caught in the middle.

"Give me your pistol," I said getting to my feet. Sharon handed it over and I gave her the Uzo and a spare clip of ammunition.

"What are you going to do?" she asked.

"Give me five minutes," I said. "I'm going to come up through the stuffing box compartment. When I open fire from below, it will draw their attention away from this doorway and you can catch them from behind."

She nodded uncertainly after a moment, leaned forward and kissed me on the cheek. "Good luck," she said.

"You too," I said, peeking around the doorframe of the engine room. The four men still had their backs to us, and without any further hesitation I slipped quietly across the opening and then hurried noiselessly down the companionway where I pulled up the section of decking and slipped down onto the catwalk.

Before I ducked out of sight, I looked down at Sharon who smiled at me and waved, then I pulled the grating closed, hunched over and hurried beneath the companionway, passing under Sharon and coming finally to the ladder that led down into the bilges.

I stuffed the pistol in my pocket and started down the ladder into the darkness. At the bottom, in water up to my knees I pulled the flashlight out, switched it on and headed aft.

My legs were numb from the icy water by the time I made it to the stuffing box compartment and pulled myself up through the hatch.

Nothing had been disturbed in our absence, but I paid that only a slight attention as I hurried across the compartment and climbed up the ladder. Carefully, so as to make no noise, I eased the wrecking bar that Sharon had used to jam the lock in the upper hatch out of place and brought it back down to the deck.

Once again at the hatch, I switched off the

flashlight, stuffed it in my pocket and pulled out the pistol.

Slowly I undogged the hatch, took a deep breath, letting it out slowly, then slammed open the hatch.

The four Russians were still at the control board, and the one with the walkie-talkie was the first to look my way.

I shot him in the chest before he could even lower the communicator, and an instant later Sharon opened fire with the Uzo from above.

It was over in less than ten seconds, not one of the Soviet troops even touching his weapon let alone returning the fire.

I climbed up out of the stuffing box compartment as Sharon hurried down from the companionway. We would have to work very fast now. It would not take very long for someone topside to come below and investigate what was going on.

At the control board I studied the dials for a moment. We were going to have to do more than just shut the engines down. Somehow we were going to have to wreck them so that they could not be repaired here at sea.

Sharon was coming across the engine room toward me when the sound of automatic-weapons fire started up out in the companionway. Someone shouted something, and seconds later what sounded like a dozen men came clattering down the companionway.

We had just run out of time.

FOURTEEN

Sharon leaped behind one of the generator units and I slipped around the back of the control panel as a black-suited figure darted across the opening above. A second later another man clad in a black jumpsuit flashed across the opening.

"Lay your weapons down," someone shouted in very bad Russian. "Your comrades are dead or captured! Lay your weapons down!"

"*Whiteshark?*" I shouted up in English.

There was silence in the companionway for several long seconds, but then the man shouted down to us in English, "Nick Carter? Is that you?"

It could be a trick, I thought, but I shouted up, "Yes," and Arnold Jacobs, the *Whiteshark*'s chief of maintenance, stepped into the doorway, a huge grin on his face.

"Thought you were dead," he said, as I stepped away from the control panel.

"Am I ever glad to see you," I said.

Jacobs issued several rapid-fire orders to his men in the companionway and then he started down to us, followed a moment later by a half a dozen others.

Sharon got up from where she had been

crouched behind the generator unit, and when Jacobs reached the bottom of the ladder and turned around, he stopped in his tracks. He looked from me to her and back to me again.

"Israeli?" he asked.

"Yes," I answered. "Did David Hawk come aboard?"

"He's topside," Jacobs said. His men came across the engine room and began adjusting controls on the panel.

"How about the *Akai Maru*'s crew?"

Jacobs shook his head. "They all bought it. Every one of them. We would have gotten here sooner but we were sort of busy with the Soviet destroyer out there. She had antisubmarine warfare capabilities, so we had to be a little careful." He had been looking at Sharon when he said all that.

"What about the gunboat?" she asked.

Jacobs seemed uncomfortable.

"What is it, chief?" I asked.

He looked at me. "The Soviets sunk her before we could do anything about it."

"No," Sharon cried. "My brother—"

"Your brother was aboard?" I interrupted.

She looked at me, anguish in her eyes. "Simon—he was a gunner's mate."

"Any survivors?" I asked.

Jacobs shook his head. "She was hit with a pair of surface-to-surface missiles. There was nothing left."

"No," Sharon screamed. Her knees gave way under her and before either of us could reach her, she collapsed on the deck.

I reached her first and cradled her in my arms. Her eyes were fluttering and she was moaning her brother's name over and over again.

Jacobs pulled out a walkie-talkie and keyed it. "This is Jacobs in the engine room. Get a couple of medics and a stretcher down here on the double," he snapped.

"She just fainted," I said.

Jacobs nodded. "I know, but we'll take her up to sick bay anyway. Looks like you could use a little attention yourself."

"Yeah," I said. "Radio up to Hawk. Tell him we've got to talk immediately. It's urgent," I said.

"Yes, sir," Jacobs said.

"One other thing," I said. I was suddenly very tired.

"Sir?" Jacobs asked, looking down at me.

"Have someone take an accurate body count."

"Are we looking for someone specific?"

"A non-Japanese. Name of Quanrum. He's one of the terrorists. I think he jumped ship, but he may still be aboard."

"We'll find him," Jacobs said.

"This ship is loaded with plastique," I heard myself saying from a distance. "Pressure sensitive. Along the holds at the bilge level. If he's still aboard he may try to set one of them off. Sink us. Spill the oil."

"Don't worry, Mr. Carter, we'll find him. I'll get the bomb disposal team on it right away."

The bullet would have to remain in my leg, the doctor told me, until I was brought aboard the aircraft carrier Ranger, which was steaming toward a rendezvous with us at this moment.

Before I left the dispensary to go up to the

captain's cabin to see Hawk, my leg was reban-
daged, and I was given a pain killer and a fresh set
of coveralls.

Sharon had been given a light sedative and was
sleeping soundly in one of the bunks. She didn't
move when I checked in on her and kissed her
cheek.

After this mission was over she would be returning to Tel Aviv to make her own report, and I knew
I would probably never see her again. Before that
happened, though, I wanted to talk to her, tell her
that without her help we would not have gotten as
far as we had. If it had not been for her, I would be
dead at this moment.

The companionway outside of the dispensary
was filled with three rows of body bags. The bodies
in one long row were tagged with the names of the
Akai Maru's crew, one even longer row with the
Soviet shock troops, and a third, smaller row,
tagged with the names of the *Whiteshark* crewmen
who had fallen.

As I headed through the makeshift morgue and
started up the stairs to the top deck, I kept thinking
about Kobelev, code-named the Puppet Master.
Despite the fact that his plot had failed, dozens of
people were now dead for no reason at all. The Soviet Union had gained nothing by his plan.

Even in failure, however, the thought struck me
as I continued up the stairs, that Kobelev had covered himself. I finally understood why he had used
the strontium 90 from the Israeli nuclear depot.

If the plan were to fail, Kobelev knew that we
would never make it public because we did not
want to create trouble for the Israelis with her ene-
mies. If the strontium 90 that had been dumped in
the oil had come from the Soviet Union, we could

have exposed the plot to the world press and the Kremlin would have had to do some very fancy back pedaling. It would have hurt their operations for years to come.

But Kobelev had been too smart for that, too smart and insanely ruthless.

I also knew that this operation was only the beginning, as far as he was concerned. There would be other plots, other plans masterminded by him, unless he was stopped permanently.

Hawk, Farmington and a couple of the other officers from the *Whiteshark* were hunched over a map spread out on the desk in the captain's cabin. When I opened the door they all looked up, relief evident on Hawk's face.

"Come in, Nick," he said.

I entered the room, closing the door softly behind me. Farmington and the others nodded my way.

"How do you feel?" Hawk asked.

"Tired," I said. "Have they found Quanrum?"

"He's not aboard as far as we can tell," Farmington said. "But the bombs have all been defused and removed. There were four set in place by your Israeli friend."

I nodded. "They thought the strontium 90 was still in its canister."

Farmington looked over at Hawk who smiled stiffly. "You were right, sir," the submarine captain said.

Hawk did not reply. "How is the woman?" he asked me.

"She's sleeping," I said. "Her brother was a gunners mate aboard the gunboat. She took it hard."

"I see," Hawk said.

I came across the room to the desk. "I'm sorry I made such a mess of this, sir—" I began, but Hawk cut me off.

"We'll talk in more detail later," he said. "For now we're trying to decide what to do with the oil."

"You know then?" I said.

Hawk nodded. "Farmington's boys found the lead-lined grease drum at one of the valve engineering stations."

"Empty?" I asked.

"It's a sophisticated piece of equipment," Farmington said. "The strontium 90 was brought aboard in the drum which is equipped with a pressure siphoning system. They dumped the material into the oil hold probably at the time of loading."

"If it wasn't for you, this ship would have been sunk and the contaminated oil spilled into the ocean. It would have been a disaster we never would have recovered from," Hawk said.

I looked down at the map which was of the Gulf section of the United States. "Any ideas for getting rid of the oil?" I asked.

"One," Hawk said. "There are a number of salt domes in Louisiana's bayous, right along the Gulf Coast. There's already five hundred million barrels of oil stored in several of them. We're going to dump the oil from this ship into one of them. Six miles deep."

"A hundred years from now the strontium 90's radioactivity will have died down to nearly negligible levels and the oil will be safe to use," Farmington said.

It was over. There was nothing left to worry about and the relief must have been evident on my face, because the brief flicker of a smile crossed Hawk's features.

"Gentlemen," he said to the others a moment later. "This mission will be classified top secret. It will not be discussed with anyone at any time, not even amongst yourselves. The President, I'm sure, will be instructing you in this matter himself. Do I make myself perfectly clear?"

"Aye aye, sir," Farmington said. The other officers nodded.

"When you get the radio link with the *Whiteshark*'s communications facilities set up, I'll want a patch to the President, Newt."

"Yes, sir," Farmington said. "Should be ready within the hour."

"Fine," Hawk said. "I'll want to get underway as soon as we've rendezvoused with the Ranger."

"You're staying aboard?"

"For now," Hawk said. "And now if you will leave us?"

"Aye aye," Farmington said, and he and the others left the cabin, closing the door firmly behind them.

Hawk took a seat behind the desk and motioned for me to sit down. He poured a half a glass of brandy for me from a bottle behind the desk and then pulled a package of my specially blended cigarettes from his pocket and tossed them across along with a book of matches.

"Thought you might have run out by now," he said.

I took a deep breath and let it out slowly, something I had been doing a lot of in the last couple of hours. Then I opened the cigarettes, lit myself one and took a sip of the brandy.

For a long time we just looked at each other. Hawk had poured himself a small brandy and had re-lit his ever-present cigar. I finally broke the silence.

"Was Kobelev behind this?"

"I think so," he said. "We'll never be sure, of course. But it has all the earmarks of a Kobelev scheme. You did a good job."

I looked away. "What's the casualty list? Fifty? Sixty?"

"One hundred and twelve," Hawk said softly. "It could have been worse. Much worse. Our analysts estimated ten million deaths in the first five years, mostly from starvation, if the oil had been spilled into the Atlantic."

I took another deep drag from the cigarette, the smoke making me somewhat lightheaded, and then took another drink of the brandy. I knew I should not be drinking on top of the pain killer, but after being shot at, nearly thrown overboard, nearly blown up and cracked on the head several times, a shot of brandy mixed with a pain killer seemed somewhat mild.

"I'm going after him," I said at long last.

Hawk's left eyebrow rose as he set his brandy glass down. "Quanrum is nowhere aboard, according to Farmington's people."

"I mean Kobelev."

"Impossible," Hawk said waving it aside.

"He has to be stopped. I'm going to do it."

"I said it was impossible," Hawk snapped impatiently. "He's under constant guard in the middle of Moscow. You got into the city once, you'll never do it again."

I held my silence for a full minute and when I

spoke, I chose my words with care. "I've never defied you before, sir," I said. "Over the years I've given you my best. But I am going after Kobelev. I was given the N3 Killmaster status. I'm going to use it. I'm going to assassinate the man."

"You're a fool, Nick," Hawk said, the words hurtful. "But you're a capable fool. And no matter what I say or do, I believe you actually will try to get Kobelev."

"Yes, sir," I said softly.

"Then AXE will help. Just give me a little time to sell it to the President."

EPILOGUE

It was decided that the Japanese shipowners could be told nothing. Once the contaminated oil was off-loaded in the Louisiana salt dome, the tanker would be taken back out to sea and sunk.

The Israelis, of course, agreed immediately to the plan, but it would be a long time before relations between Israel and the United States normalized.

Nuclear capability was now a fact of life in the Middle East, and the CIA was going to have its hands full watching the Arab bloc countries for any sign of retaliation.

It had long been Hawk's contention that if a nuclear war was ever to start, it would begin in the Middle East.

"Frankly, I'm concerned about it," Hawk told me before I left him in the captain's quarters. "But it's out of our hands now. The politicians will have to work it out."

My weapons had been found locked in the captain's desk, and Hawk handed them over to me.

"Don't worry about it, Nick," he said gently. "You did a fine job under the circumstances."

"Yeah," I said morosely. I was thinking of Sakai

at the bottom of the access tunnel.

"Get some rest now. We'll be transferring over to the Ranger in about twelve hours."

"Yes, sir," I said, and I left the cabin and headed back down to the dispensary.

The *Whiteshark*'s maintenance crew had already fixed the helm control that I had jimmied, and the bridge was alive with activity, much of the equipment the doctor and his people had wrecked already repaired.

Barring any other catastrophe, the *Akai Maru* would make it to the Louisiana coast within a few days. It would be her very last voyage.

They were just bringing Sakai's body to the makeshift morgue when I made it to the dispensary, and I stopped to watch a moment as they checked for a pulse before they declared him officially dead. His pockets were emptied, the contents placed in a manila envelope and his body was stuffed in a long rubber bag, tagged with his name and placed in the long row with the other crewmen.

Most of the wounded had been taken care of and things were beginning to settle down in the dispensary as I crossed the main room to look in on Sharon.

"If you're looking for the woman, she's not there," one of the medics said to me, looking up from his work.

"Where'd she go?" I asked, opening the door anyway and looking inside. The bed she had been sleeping in was empty, the covers thrown back.

"Said something about getting her things," the medic said.

"Why didn't you stop her?" I snapped.

"She wasn't wounded, and we were kinda' busy,

sir," the Navy medic said.

"Sorry," I apologized. "I'll bring her back here and you can give her a heavier sedative. She needs sleep."

"Aye aye, sir," the young man said.

I left the dispensary, crossed to the aft companionway and limped down the stairs. Hawk and I had talked for at least two hours and the pain killer the doctor had given me for the wound in my leg was starting to wear off. Once I had Sharon back in the dispensary, I was going to have to get off my feet for some much needed rest before I collapsed.

Jacobs and three of his men were in the engine room where they had started up a poker game on a crate set up in front of the control panel.

When I came down the ladder he looked up and grinned. "How about a little not so friendly game of poker, Mr. Carter," he said.

"Later, chief," I said coming across the room to him. "Have you seen the woman?"

He glanced over toward the open hatch that led down into the stuffing box compartment. "She just came through here about five minutes ago. Said her things were down there."

"Thanks," I said tiredly, and I went over to the hatch and looked inside.

Sharon was sitting on her sleeping bag looking at a photograph. She was crying.

"Sharon?" I said, and I climbed down the ladder into the tiny compartment.

She looked up. "He was only nineteen," she said.

I took the photograph from her and looked at the handsome young man smiling at the camera. He was dressed in Navy whites.

"I don't know how I'm going to tell my mother —" she started to say when her eyes went wide. "Nick!" she screamed.

I spun around as Quanrum, covered with oil, came up out of the hatch from the bilge. He had a wild, gruesome expression on his face as he brought a pistol up and fired it twice.

I leaped to the left, pulling out my Luger. I snapped a round in the chamber, thumbed the safety off and fired, hitting him in the forehead.

He dropped his pistol as his head snapped back, and then fell down into the bilge with a splash.

"Sharon—" I started to say as I turned around, but the words died in my throat.

"What the hell is going on?" Jacobs shouted from above, as I went to where Sharon was lying on her back, her eyes open. The front of her clean white coveralls was splattered with blood. One bullet had caught her in the chest just above her left breast and the other had caught her in the face to the right of her nose.

She must have died instantly.

I dropped down beside her and cradled her in my arms as Jacobs and his men clambered down the ladder into the stuffing box compartment.

"Where in hell did he come from?" Jacobs was shouting.

I looked up at him. "He was hiding in the hold," I said.

"In the oil?" Jacobs said. "Jesus," he swore, and he began issuing orders for the radiation cleanup crew to get down here on the double. Quanrum's body would be hot and would have to be handled with care.

As I held Sharon in my arms and looked down at

her destroyed face, I kept thinking one man's name. It ran through my brain over and over again like a broken record in time with a rising, bleak anger.

Kobelev. Nikolai Fedor Kobelev.

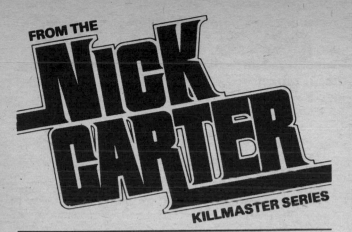